something like fate

something like fate

SUSANE
COLASANTI

VIKING
An Imprint of Penguin Group (USA) Inc.

VIKING
Published by Penguin Group
Penguin Group (USA) Inc., 345 Hudson Street, New York, New York 10014, U.S.A.
Penguin Group (Canada), 90 Eglinton Avenue East, Suite 700, Toronto, Ontario, Canada M4P 2Y3
(a division of Pearson Penguin Canada Inc.)
Penguin Books Ltd, 80 Strand, London WC2R 0RL, England
Penguin Ireland, 25 St Stephen's Green, Dublin 2, Ireland (a division of Penguin Books Ltd)
Penguin Group (Australia), 250 Camberwell Road, Camberwell, Victoria 3124, Australia
(a division of Pearson Australia Group Pty Ltd)
Penguin Books India Pvt Ltd, 11 Community Centre, Panchsheel Park, New Delhi – 110 017, India
Penguin Group (NZ), 67 Apollo Drive, Rosedale, North Shore 0632, New Zealand
(a division of Pearson New Zealand Ltd)
Penguin Books (South Africa) (Pty) Ltd, 24 Sturdee Avenue, Rosebank, Johannesburg 2196, South Africa

Penguin Books Ltd, Registered Offices: 80 Strand, London WC2R 0RL, England

First published in the U.S.A. by Viking, a member of Penguin Group (USA) Inc., 2010

1   3   5   7   9   10   8   6   4   2

Copyright © Susane Colasanti, 2010
All rights reserved

LIBRARY OF CONGRESS CATALOGING-IN-PUBLICATION DATA
Colasanti, Susane.
Something like fate / by Susane Colasanti.
p. cm.
Summary: Lani and Jason, who is her best friend's boyfriend, fall in love,
causing Lani tremendous anguish and guilt.
ISBN 978-0-670-01146-9 (hardcover)
[1. Interpersonal relations—Fiction. 2. Guilt—Fiction. 3. Friendship—Fiction. 4. Schools—Fiction.]
I. Title.
PZ7.C6699So 2010
[Fic]—dc22
2009024906

Printed in U.S.A.   Set in Minion   Book design by Jim Hoover

Without limiting the rights under copyright reserved above, no part of this publication may be reproduced, stored in or introduced into a retrieval system, or transmitted, in any form or by any means (electronic, mechanical, photocopying, recording or otherwise), without the prior written permission of both the copyright owner and the above publisher of this book. The scanning, uploading, and distribution of this book via the Internet or via any other means without the permission of the publisher is illegal and punishable by law. Please purchase only authorized electronic editions, and do not participate in or encourage electronic piracy of copyrighted materials. Your support of the author's rights is appreciated.

The publisher does not have any control over and does not assume any responsibility for author or third-party Web sites or their content.

This is a work of fiction. Names, characters, places, and incidents either are the product of the author's imagination or are used fictitiously, and any resemblance to actual persons, living or dead, businesses, companies, events, or locales is entirely coincidental.

For Shawn,

inventor of the note code,

however far away

something like fate

part one

april–may

"If you believe in coincidence,
then you aren't paying attention."
                    —David Life

"The pleasure of what we enjoy
is lost by wanting more."
                    —fortune cookie

1

I never meant for it to happen like this. But if I had the chance, there's no way I would take it all back.

2

"Why are you always checking your horoscope?" Blake accuses.

"Why aren't *you*?" I say. Checking my weekly horoscope every Monday is an essential part of my life. It's like, took a shower, check. Went to school, check. Did homework, partial check (depending on the length of work involved and difficulty level). Today is Monday, so read horoscope, definite check.

He goes, "Um, I don't know, maybe because it's bogus?"

I gasp. The gasp is half joking and half serious. "Take that back!"

"No."

"Take it back!"

"Not until you prove that horoscopes aren't a totally bogus waste of time."

"Like that'll be difficult." I grab my laptop, which is sliding off the pillow. When I'm online, I like to sit on my bed. But when I'm doing homework, I sit at my desk. My bed is a relaxation-only zone.

"Go ahead, then," Blake challenges.

"Fine, I will." I'm on the best website for weekly horoscopes. I don't know how this astrologer does it, but she's scarily accurate every single week. She just *knows*. True, I've only been checking the site since school started, and it's April. So that's like . . . thirty horoscopes. Which I think is enough to know that my horoscope is something I can trust. It helps me feel prepared for whatever happens next. Sort of.

I'm not a fan of the Unknown. The Unknown can change your entire life in an instant. The Unknown can take everything away from you and never give it back. Your life can end in a flash before you even have time to know it's over.

There is no safe. There is no control.

I scroll down the page, searching. "Oh! Here." I scroll down some more. "'Mars and the creative Uranus synergistically merge their energies on the ninth, exposing you to an exciting world of possibilities. Mars, the ruler of ambition, is turning your life around and will be pushing you over new thresholds and into new situations. If you continue to cling to your comfortable routine, you could miss out on new people, interesting ideas, and' . . . yeah."

"And yeah what?" Blake says.

"And just . . . whatever, the rest didn't go."

"Aha!"

"That is *so* not the point. Everything else totally goes!"

"So then why doesn't the last part go?"

"Because it's about professional possibilities. It's for people with jobs."

"See? You don't *have* a job."

"Because I'm in school!"

"Exactly!"

"What, like I'm the only Taurus who's sixteen? We're all different ages!"

"Uh-huh."

"What about the rest of it? How do you explain how perfect all that other stuff is?"

"Riiight. Because new opportunities are only happening to you."

"That's not . . . forget it." It's not just about what my horoscope says. It's about astrology in general. I definitely believe that whatever sign you are determines your inherent personality traits. I totally fit the description of a Taurus: loves nature, seeks comfort and pleasure, connects with the Earth, into serenity, stubborn, passionate, and nurturing. It's a quality sign.

"Aw." Blake sits on my bed. "Don't get all offended."

"I'm not," I say. But I am. I'm sensitive about people blowing off the things I believe in like they're nothing. Like I'm this freak who's confusing fantasy with reality.

People who don't get astrology are always like, *Why do you even care what your horoscope says? Why don't you just live your life?* The thing is, if you know what to look out for, you can be ready for anything. Well, maybe not anything, but you can be ready for things you wouldn't normally be ready for if you didn't know about them. It helps me deal with the Unknown.

Blake scrunches up next to me. He's like, "What does mine say?"

There are a few people in my life I can always count on. Blake is one of them. We've been friends for two years and we've never had a fight. The only person I'm closer to than Blake is Erin. She's been my best friend for a long time. Erin's a Leo, which means her temper can be a problem. She's also fearless and self-confident, which sometimes makes me jealous. I wouldn't call myself an introvert, but I wish I were as outgoing as Erin. I'd give anything to know what it feels like to be fearless.

Blake is awesome. He's so funny. And super reliable. He's never let me down, not even once. Plus, he's really cute. But not in a way where I'm attracted to him. Well, maybe I would be if he weren't gay.

No one else knows. If Blake were any farther back in the closet, he'd have random Boy Scout camping equipment and shirts he outgrew in middle school piled on top of him. Blake's dad would kill him if knew he was gay. For real. So Blake's not coming out until college, when he says his real life will start. He spends a lot of time on school stuff so his transcript will open doors to wherever he wants to go. He's always talking about how amazing college will be—when he can be his true self, without worrying about impending death by deranged parent.

Things might be different if his mom were still here, but

she married some other guy when Blake was thirteen. Then she moved to California. At first, she called Blake all the time. Now Blake only hears from her on his birthday.

Everyone assumes Blake is straight. He likes blending in. It's just easier that way. Besides me, he only hangs out with a couple other friends. Kids at school see us together all the time. I even heard a rumor that we were going out. Blake considers this a compliment because he insists that I'm a "hot babe." Whenever he calls me that, I laugh so hard. I don't think I'm hot at all. Unless you consider short and skinny to be hot. I wish I were taller with more curves, like Erin. My hazel-blue eyes hardly make me more attractive. Neither does my straight, black hair, even though it's long. I wear it with bangs to cover the scar on my forehead. Trust me. There's nothing sexy about a ripped-up face.

I totally think Blake would be out if it weren't for his dad. It's not that Blake wants to hide who he is. He doesn't even care that much what other kids think. He just doesn't want to deal with his dad finding out. The fights they have are seriously scary. Blake's dad never hits him or anything (which might change if he knew), but I've heard his dad yell. Some of the things he's said probably hurt worse than anything physical ever could.

Blake trusted me with the truth last summer when we were spending all this time together. It was obvious that something major was going on with him. I swore that I wouldn't tell anyone. Erin doesn't even know.

I click on "Capricorn" so we can read Blake's horoscope.

"There!" I yell. "What does the second paragraph say?"

"Yeah, yeah . . ."

"That wasn't a rhetorical question."

"You're very demanding today."

"You love it. Now read."

Blake reads. "'Hiding behind your protective layer is wearing you down. With the moon in dramatic Leo, you're inspired to launch a personal crusade to support your future ambitions. Keep your eye on the prize and continue handling unrewarding arrangements with calm determination. When the dust settles, you will prevail in a domestic or personal transaction.'"

I'm like, "Now what have we learned?"

"Hmph." I can tell Blake is fighting it. He has to admit there's something legit going on here.

"Doesn't it make you feel better about things?"

"I'm not particularly motivated to go out and launch a personal crusade yet. Maybe this applies to a year from now?"

"It can be for whenever you want."

"Let's ask Magic 8 Ball," Blake says. I have a special glittery Magic 8 Ball. We always consult it for matters of importance. "Is it time for me to launch a personal crusade?" he asks. Then he shakes Magic 8 Ball and turns it over. "'My sources say no.'"

"It does *not* say that!"

"Yuh-huh!" Blake shoves Magic 8 Ball at me.

"Okay, well . . . like I said, it can be for whenever."

I just hope that whenever gets here soon. Blake should be living the life he wants.

3

Erin is in love.

"Who's the boy?" I ask.

"What boy?" she goes. I don't know why she bothers pretending. She knows I know there's a boy. I can always tell.

I'm like, "The boy you're in love with."

Now that Erin's scored the glossy new Beetle convertible she's been lusting after forever (in heaven blue, which is a seriously sweet color), I don't have to wait for Mom to pick me up after school. I love the feeling of riding home with Erin, like we're totally free, like we can go anywhere. Her Beetle gets about twenty-four miles per gallon. This could be better, so I only partially approve of its efficiency. But I absolutely approve of the cute flower holder, which I keep filled with flowers from my garden.

Since Erin got her car, she's been great about driving me home. Everything's so spread out in our town. Some people take walks, but just when they feel like walking. They don't actually get anywhere. I'll ride my bike to go somewhere nearby, but you need a car to get anywhere real. When Erin gives me a ride home, it takes her all this extra time to go from my house to hers. Good thing she's so into her car. Any excuse to drive it works for her.

"There's no boy," Erin says. She has this secret smile and faraway eyes. It's obvious there's a boy.

"Oh," I say, "there's a boy."

"Well." More faraway eyes. "There *might* be a boy."

"If there was a boy, what would his name be?"

"Jason."

I've had a few classes with Jason, but I've never really talked to him. He's in Erin's multimedia elective. She was lusting after him so hard when spring semester started, but she couldn't figure out what to do about it. Then they got put together for a group project and started talking.

Actually, they were talking a little before that. They have a big group of mutual friends. I call it the Golden Circle. It's the same group I used to be in, but that was before it absorbed Jason and some other kids I don't really know. I'd still be part of that group if I were the same joiner I used to be. Oh, and if Bianca didn't have that tizzy fit last year.

I don't know what her problem was. I guess she noticed that I was gradually drifting away from everyone. It wasn't like a conscious decision or anything. I just didn't feel like doing as much group stuff anymore. Especially since it felt like the same parties at the same houses with the same hundred people. My connections with them started to seem so superficial.

Bianca took offense.

"Why are you being like this?" she went. A bunch of us were hanging out after school at Green Pond, just goofing off and wasting time. I was getting bored. I found a big rock jutting out over the pond and went to sit there alone. Bianca followed me.

"Being like what?" I asked.

"You're acting like you're better than us."

"No I'm not."

"Then why didn't you come out with us last weekend?"

"I just didn't feel like it."

"Why not?"

"I don't know. I didn't realize it was a required activity." I had no idea why Bianca was harassing me. She was getting more annoying every day.

Bianca was all, "Since when don't you feel like hanging out with your friends?"

"It's not like that. I'm here, aren't I?"

"Yeah, but are you having a good time?"

"Where is all this coming from? Did I do something?"

"You think you're too good to be around people who aren't activists or whatever."

"No I don't!"

"Just because we're not out saving the environment doesn't mean we're losers," Bianca huffed. "We do a lot for the school, you know."

The Golden Kids have a reputation for being friendly and helpful. They do a zillion school activities. They've completely taken over the student council. A few of them mentor at the middle school, which Erin's been thinking about doing. They're all popular, but not crazy popular like the jocks. They're sort of all the kids who are lucky enough to have both decent looks and decent home lives. Which means they also have a decent amount of money to play with. I'd rather have my parents save money to help me with college, so I'm not into the Golden Kids' materialistic ways.

But it makes sense that Erin's still friends with them. She loves volunteering, especially with little kids. Erin was a candy striper in the pediatric ward at the hospital for a long time. She's the best babysitter. She even has a bag of tricks that she brings over when she babysits. She's completely not embarrassed to still like all the fun stuff we were into when we were eight. Kids love Erin as much as she loves them.

Anyway. After that confrontation with Bianca, I basically stopped doing stuff with the group, except for Erin. I'd still talk to everyone if they talked to me, but after a while they stopped.

It's interesting how you can know someone for a long time, and then one day you just see them in this whole different way. That's clearly what happened to Erin with Jason.

"I think he likes me," Erin gushes.

"Cool."

"Everyone's been pushing us to get together, so they must have a reason."

"Maybe he told someone he likes you and now they all know."

"You think so?"

"Totally."

"Of course we got put together for multimedia. The Energy is bringing us together."

I definitely believe everything happens for a reason. I'm just not sure I believe Erin's reason for why she got put with Jason.

Erin's all, "Jason stayed after yesterday to ask me about something he totally could have found out from anyone. But he asked *me*!"

"Because he obviously likes you."

"Really?"

"Of course. Why else would he ask you?"

"I know!" Erin's cheeks get pink. "He is *so* cute."

"Yeah."

"You think he's cute?" Erin thinks I can get any boy I want. She's seriously delusional. The boys who approach me are usually obnoxious types who dedicate their lives to picking on anyone even remotely different from them. Like that's attractive.

Erin knows that we could never be interested in the same boy. Not that I'd ever go after him if I were. But it would be impossible for me to like a boy she likes. We have totally different types.

I go, "He's cute for you, I mean."

"Really?"

"Totally."

"All signs point to us being together. I had a dream where I was eating this huge ice-cream cone. You know what ice cream represents?"

We always interpret our dreams. Erin believes that symbolism in dreams foretells the future. I'm more into the kind of dream analysis where you interpret how the symbolism relates to your current situation.

We're both obsessed with fate. Anything that helps us make sense of this life is fascinating. At the beginning of the year we made a chart. The chart has topics related to fate that we want to know more about. Each topic has its own month. During that month, we learn as much as we can and have these intense discussions about everything we find out. By the end of this year, we'll be experts on fate.

Here's our chart:

Erin & Lani's Fate Study Chart—Junior Year

September	Numerology
October	Graphology
November	Birth charts/moon signs
December	Creative visualization
January	Buddhism/Taoism
February	Shamanism
March	Dream analysis
April	Tarot
May	Palmistry
June	Gemology

Even though we were just learning about dream analysis, I can't remember what ice cream represents. Or if I even learned that one. It's impossible to memorize the meanings of more than a few symbols. We decided that the key to dream analysis is checking a reliable website or book after every dream.

"I don't remember that one," I go.

"It symbolizes compensating for lack of contentment and foretells that the best is yet to come. Oh! The ice cream was this rusty orange color? And the next day Jason was wearing a shirt that exact same color!"

"Get out."

"Well, it was almost the same color." Erin tells me more about Jason and how she thinks he likes her but how she doesn't know for sure so she's going to wait and see if he asks her out.

"Do you think that's a good idea?" she wants to know.

"Yeah. Or you could always initiate things."

"But isn't it better to wait for him to ask me out?"

"It is, but don't wait too long. What if he asks someone else out because he doesn't know you like him?"

"If he likes me, he shouldn't be asking anyone else out!"

"I know. I'm just saying if he doesn't do anything soon, you might want to."

If we weren't so close, I might be jealous that Erin has a boy to like and I don't. But I just feel happy for her. Erin and I are bonded for life. Being bonded for life isn't the same as being best friends. I mean, we're best friends, but it goes way beyond that. What do you call it when two people have an intense shared history? When nothing can ever separate them? Soul sisters. That's what we've been ever since the accident.

Except lately I can feel things changing. It's like we're growing apart or something. The weird thing is, this somehow happened when I wasn't looking. There's not really any one thing I can say is the reason we're drifting. Maybe that's just what happens when you grow up. My parents hardly know anyone they went to high school with. How is that possible? Do you graduate and then just let your friends fade away? Even when they seem like your whole world?

I know that won't happen with Erin. I love being so close to another person, knowing that our connection will always be there. It makes me feel safe. Only . . . if I were going to be really honest with myself, I would have to admit that we're not the same Erin and Lani we were before. I can't tell how much of our connection is because of the things we still have in common or the one thing that bonds us for life.

But no matter what happens, I know I can totally count on Erin for anything. And she knows I'd do anything for her.

4

I'm trying not to spill more paint. So far, I've made five signs and spilled blue paint on my floor. At least my house has hardwood floors, so it wasn't impossible to clean up.

To make this sign for the cafeteria recycling bins, I'm using bold colors and big letters. I'm also putting on glitter and outlining the letters in metallic markers. I want to make it impossible for people not to notice the bin labeled BOTTLES & CANS. I'm so over kids using the tired excuse that they didn't see the sign every time they throw their water bottles in the garbage can. With my new signs, no one will have an excuse not to recycle.

Marnie and Bianca were supposed to help me make the signs, but they canceled at the last minute. I wish they weren't in our club. It's so obvious they're just using it to put on their college apps. Danielle came over for a few hours, though. We became really good friends after I broke away from the Golden Circle. These days I have more in common with Danielle than Erin. She's the only other person at school who cares as much about saving the planet as I do.

I'm president of One World, our school's environmental club. A junior gets to be president for two years, so at the end of next year we'll vote for a new president. I guess you could say my love for Earth is genetic. My mom's an environmental-health specialist and my dad builds greenhouses. They obviously have the environmental thing in common, but Mom is fifteen years younger than Dad. So that's where the similarity ends. Dad's ultimate night involves sitting at home working on a cross-word puzzle or reading a mystery novel. Mom's all about the social life. She loves meeting new people and getting the word out about green living. We even have an organic garden in our backyard. Mom sells vegetables from it at the green market every summer.

Everyone in town knows my mom. We live in one of those small New Jersey towns that's close to a lot of other small New Jersey towns called things like Tranquility and Peapack and Glad-stone. Everyone tends to know everyone else in towns like these. So my friends are used to Mom's house rules. When they come over, they always turn off the lights when they leave a room. They never let the water run when they're not using it. We also have to unplug the TV and computer when we're done with them, be-cause when they're left plugged in they still use electricity, even when they're turned off.

One thing I like about my house is that there's tons of natural light, so we usually don't turn on lamps during the day. It has a lot of glass and high ceilings and open spaces. We have three skylights and two sets of sliding-glass doors—one for the upstairs balcony and one for the back porch. The back porch leads out to a dock with Dad's rowboat tied to it. Sometimes he rows out to the middle of the lake and does his crossword puzzles there.

An entire container of glitter just spilled all over the place. Educating the public is never easy.

Somehow I manage to finish the sign without spilling anything else. Then I lean it up against the wall to dry. My computer dings with an IM. It's from Erin.

aceofwands: omg you are NOT going to believe this!!!

berrygirl: what?

aceofwands: jason called me!

berrygirl: shut up!

aceofwands: i gave him my number in class today. we just got off the phone.

berrygirl: details please.

aceofwands: he wanted to know if i did the homework yet. he said he had a question on it, which we all know is code for he wants me.

berrygirl: did it even sound like a real question?

aceofwands: hells no! and that's not all. i think he's going to ask me out.

berrygirl: how do you know?

aceofwands: just a feeling. oh, and i told him i like him.

berrygirl: what happened to waiting for him to come to you?

aceofwands: i did! he's the one who called me, remember? so i was like, okay, he's putting himself out there, i can meet the boy halfway.

berrygirl: what did you say?

aceofwands: i was just like how i think he's cute. and funny ☺

berrygirl: and?

aceofwands: and he said he had no idea i felt that way.

berrygirl: boys are so clueless.

aceofwands: tell me about it. but now he knows. so it's just a matter of time.

berrygirl: you go with your fine self.

aceofwands: thanks, i will. what about you?

berrygirl: ?

aceofwands: with greg?!

berrygirl: how many times do I have to tell you this? i. do. not. like. greg.

aceofwands: why not?

berrygirl: *headdesk* um, i don't know, maybe because we have absolutely nothing in common? at ALL?

aceofwands: oh. that.

berrygirl: why do you always act like i never told you this?

aceofwands: i'm not sure. maybe for the same reason you always act like he's not the most gorgeous slice of boy you've ever seen?

berrygirl: like that's the most important thing.

aceofwands: it doesn't hurt.

berrygirl: and it doesn't help when we have nothing to talk about.

aceofwands: who's talking about talking?

berrygirl: slut.

aceofwands: stop talking trash about yourself.

berrygirl: gotta go . . . more signs to do.

aceofwands: ciao for now.

I'm less than shocked that Erin went ahead and told Jason she likes him before she even knew if he liked her. When she wants something, she stays totally focused on that one thing until she gets it. She's fearless like that.

I wish I could say the same thing about myself.

5

In a school as small as ours, you know the names of everyone in your class. There are seventy-three people in our junior class. Most of us have gone to school together since first grade. But that doesn't mean we actually know one another. I know people by their reputations and who they hang out with and how they act in class. These judgments aren't based on truth. You can't ever know the real anybody unless you're friends with them. And sometimes not even then.

I don't really fit into any group. Not anymore. I like doing my own thing. I mean, I obviously relate to the other kids in One World and naturally I get labeled as a tree hugger. I'm not that easy to define, though. I'm not popular, but I'm not unpopular. I'm not a jock, but I'm not inept at sports. I'm not a nerd, but I'm not a slacker. I guess it sounds like I'm pretty average. But I'm not that, either.

It's always been hard for me to find people I can relate to. The people in One World are great, but Danielle's the only one I'm really good friends with. When I try to be friends with people I don't feel enough of a connection with, things always fizzle out. It's not worth the effort to put so much energy into building a friendship with someone if you're just going to drift apart anyway.

Erin wants me and Blake to be friends with Jason. She keeps saying how hard next year's going to rock with the four of us doing stuff together. It's like she wants us to double-date or something. Erin's excitement for senior year is scary. I'm excited too, but only because it's our last year. Erin's acting like senior year's going to be one big party with her as the guest of honor. Which totally doesn't surprise me. She loves being the center of attention. She also loves to discuss boys she likes. Specifically, whether or not these boys might like her back. I'm sure part of the reason Erin wants all of us to hang out is so we can talk about Jason after.

So we're all getting pizza. Blake can't wait to evaluate Jason. Jason's not here yet, though. We've only been waiting for ten minutes, but Erin's freaking out.

"Where *is* he?" Erin leans way over on her stool and stretches her neck out for a better view of the sidewalk. This makes me nervous. She's five nine and looks like she's about to tip over.

"Don't worry," I tell her.

"He should be here by now."

"He's only like ten minutes late."

"Exactly. He's never late."

I don't say what I want to say, which is that this is only the third time they're hanging out. You can't know what a person *never* does if you've only hung out with them two times before.

Blake's like, "All I know is, if we don't eat soon I'm going to chew off a limb. And I can't guarantee it'll be mine."

"Didn't you eat lunch?" I say.

"Not so much, no."

"Why not?"

"I wasn't hungry then."

"You are *so* manorexic."

"Which is why I'm hungry enough to eat three pizzas."

"Let's just order so it'll be ready by the time Jason gets here." I look at Erin. "Okay?"

Erin leans back toward us. "What?"

"Can we please order?" Blake begs. "I'm going to faint and what kind of fun company will I be then?"

Erin is not liking this idea. "We don't know what Jason wants."

"We're at the pizza place," Blake explains. "He wants pizza."

"Yeah, but—"

"No fighting at the table, kids," I warn. Erin must really be nervous. She and Blake usually have this thing where Blake's all adoring of Erin's fabulousness and Erin basks in the glow of his attention. They haven't even joked in their usual flirting-but-not way once the whole time we've been here. At first, Erin thought Blake liked her. She was totally freaking out because she didn't like him back. But I just told her that Blake didn't like her that way either, and then everything was fine.

"Fine," Erin says. "Order. But don't blame me when it's not what Jason wants."

"We'll get extra cheese," Blake says. "Who doesn't like extra cheese?"

Erin stretches over on her stool again. She keeps turning one of her rings. Erin wears a million rings. She always turns them when she's nervous.

"If he doesn't like extra cheese, he's not worthy," Blake mumbles to me. Then he attempts to flag down the waiter, who's sitting at a back table drinking coffee.

"There he is!" Erin squeals. Jason's crossing the street. Erin waves, but he doesn't see her. He has cool sneakers. We all watch him come over, just staring at him. I hope we're not making him uncomfortable.

"Hey," Jason says. "Sorry I'm late."

"You're late?" Erin goes. "I didn't notice."

Blake rolls his eyes.

Jason glances at us.

Erin's like, "Oh! You know Blake and Lani, right?"

"Kind of. Hey."

We say hey back.

Jason sits on the stool next to Erin. I notice that they're about the same height.

Blake's like, "You're okay with extra cheese, right?"

"I'm all about the extra cheese," Jason confirms.

"See?" Blake says to Erin, still flapping his arms wildly at the oblivious waiter. "I told you."

"You didn't think I'd want extra cheese?" Jason asks Erin. Then he makes a face like, *Who wouldn't want extra cheese?*

"No, I did, but I just said how you might want other toppings."

"I'm minimalist about pizza," Jason says. "It tastes better with less stuff on it, you know?"

Erin, who enjoys about ten toppings crammed on her pizza, goes, "Totally."

Jason looks over at me. "We had algebra together, right?"

"Yeah." That was two years ago. I only vaguely remember him. Something about circles. "Didn't you draw perfect circles?"

"That's what I'm known for."

"Really?" Erin goes, all excited about the circles.

Jason says, "No, it's just this one time I went up to the board and I had to draw a circle and it came out really . . . round."

"Which is always a good thing, when you're drawing a circle," I say.

"Exactly." Jason smiles at me.

"It was more than one time," I remind him. For some reason, it's all coming back to me now. "It was more like three or four times."

"What can I say?" Jason goes. "You got me."

Now we're both smiling.

Blake stares at us.

"So," Erin says. "What do we want to drink?"

While we're eating, Blake drills Jason with questions. It's Blake's way of making sure Jason is worthy of the magnificence that is Erin. If Jason feels like he's on the hot seat, he doesn't show it at all.

When Blake finishes his second slice and reaches for a third, I'm like, "Feeling better?"

He winks at me. "Much."

I reach over and pick a crust crumb off his lip. This always happens with Blake. He eats so quickly that part of whatever he's wolfing down usually ends up on his face.

After, it turns out that Jason and I are going the same way. Blake and Erin live in the opposite direction. Jason says he'll drive me so Erin doesn't have to. We split up and I get in Jason's car. I know that Erin's psyched about this development. I'm sure she can't wait to call me later to find out what Jason said about her.

The weird thing is, I feel really comfortable with Jason. Like I've known him for a long time. Like we're already good friends.

Jason goes, "Aren't you in my lunch?"

"Do you have lunch fifth period?"

"Yeah."

"Then I am."

"Cool."

Jason plays with the radio.

"Where do you sit?" I ask.

"Over with the other dorks and losers."

I laugh. Jason is all Golden Boy: popular, friendly, and cute. "Yeah, right. You're like the total opposite."

"How do you know? We just officially met an hour ago."

"I can tell."

"You can tell."

"Absolutely. I'm a great judge of character."

"Wow."

"Bet you didn't know that about me."

"How could I possibly know that? We just officially met—"

"—an hour ago. I remember."

Jason looks over at me and smiles. Something really intense is happening. It's so different from anything I've ever felt before that I don't even know what it is.

"So where do you live?" Jason says.

"On Lake End Road."

"Isn't that near Echo Lake?"

"Yeah. My backyard is basically the lake."

"Why do they call it that?"

"My dad says it's because if you yell across to the other side, you can hear an echo."

"Have you tried it?"

"Yeah. No echo."

"Huh. The landscape probably looked a lot different back when the lake was named."

"That's what my dad says."

Jason drives. We don't say anything for a while.

"Erin's really great," I blurt out.

"She's fun," he says.

I wait for him to talk about Erin some more. But there is no more.

I feel the need to talk about her. Not like I'm doing anything wrong—Jason's just driving me home; it's nothing—but something's bothering me.

I go, "We've been best friends for a long time."

"Yeah, she told me. You guys were in a car accident?"

I can't believe she told him that. They've only been talking for, what, not even two weeks? Okay, everyone already knows about the accident. Big news plus a small town equals everyone knowing stuff that's none of their business two seconds after it happened. But that was years ago. Most kids at school don't remember the details. I'm sure some of them have forgotten it ever happened. So Jason probably heard about it at the time, but then he forgot.

There's no way he knows the whole story. Unless Erin told him everything.

"That was a long time ago," I say. "I don't really like talking about it."

"No, totally, I shouldn't have said anything."

"No, it's okay."

When we get to my house, I go, "Thanks for the ride."

"You're welcome. Nice house, by the way."

"Thanks."

"Have you always lived here?"

"Yeah. It was my grandparents', but they moved to Florida."

"So did mine. I think there's a conspiracy with old people moving to Florida."

"I thought they liked it there because it's warm."

"Oh, it's more than that. Believe me."

I like it when Jason gets weird-funny like this, but I don't always know what to say back. I just go, "I'm sure you're right."

I can usually tell when a boy likes me. There have been a few. But the reason I've never had a boyfriend is because they all

seemed really immature. I mean, I've gone out with a few different boys, but I've always kept it casual. I just never felt the kind of
connection I've always wanted to feel.

Until now.

This is so messed up.

When Blake calls me later, he's immediately like, "I have *never*
seen a boy look at you that way."

"What way?"

"Like he wants to lick you up."

"Stop."

"Lick you up like a sweet little ice-cream cone."

"Can we *not*?"

"Like he was stranded in the desert."

"This is so messed up."

"We can't help who we like."

"I don't like him!"

"Well, he sure likes you."

"I seriously doubt that. And even if he did, there's no way he'd
do anything about it."

"Why not?"

"Because he's already going out with Erin!"

"Erin would deal. She wouldn't have a choice. Anyway, it's not
like they're official."

"You are *so* wrong about this."

"Ice-cream cone with a cherry on top."

"I'm asking Magic 8 Ball." I pick it up and say, "Does Jason
like me?" Then I shake it.

"What does it say?"

I turn it over. "'It is decidedly so.'"

"There's a news flash."

"He *doesn't*."

"You can't deny reality. So what if the reality is particularly harsh? You and I both know that this life thing is anything but easy."

There's no way Jason likes me. Even if he did, I could never like him back. What kind of person would do something like that to their best friend?

6

We're doing pottery in art this week. I kind of suck at it.

Of course, Connor rules at it. He stands next to the pottery wheel, watching me struggle.

He's like, "Try not to press in so much."

My hands are wrapped around a lump of clay that I'm spinning on the wheel. My hand-foot coordination seems to be severely lacking today. Every time I want to slow down the wheel, I press harder on the pedal. And yes, I have accepted that my only artistic talent involves making posters.

I press in the clay too much. It oozes up over my hands and flows down onto the wheel.

"Oh, well," Connor goes in his mellow tone. It's an instant stress-reliever. "Try again."

I love Connor. He has a calming effect on me in times of crisis. We had art together last year, too. Not that I wanted to take art again. We're required to take three years of creative electives. Whenever I'm having a hard time with a project, Connor swoops over to rescue me, all laid-back and helpful. He never worries about the things everyone else worries about. Maybe it has something to do with him being Canadian. He moved here in ninth grade from Montreal. He still has a strange accent and a stranger vocabulary. This one day when he was talking about gym, I had no idea what he was saying. He was trying to tell me something about his jogging pants.

I was like, "Your *what*?"

He went, "I forgot my jogging pants."

And I was all, "You mean your *sweatpants*?"

But Connor didn't know what those were.

I lump the clay together again. I smack it down on the wheel. The clay needs to know who's in charge.

"Only press down a little on the pedal," Connor advises.

"I know, I'm trying."

"So let's see."

I try again. This time, I don't crush the mug I'm trying to form.

"Looking good, eh?" he says.

"Yeah, eh." That's another thing about Connor. He totally laughs when you imitate his Canadian speech habits, like saying "eh" all the time.

Keeping my fingers together, I wrap my hands around the

sides of the clay. Then I slowly push my thumbs down into the top.

Connor goes, "A little faster is good."

I gently press my foot down on the pedal. I can feel the wheel working the way I want it to. I'm finally getting the hang of this. I pull my thumbs apart, still sinking them down into the top of the lump. As the clay spins, the place where I'm pressing my thumbs in gets wider. I can actually tell that this part is the inside of the mug.

When my mug looks like a real mug the next day, I'm stoked. I bring it over to our table and show Connor. "Check me out!" I brag.

"You rock," Connor says. He's glazing his piece. After we glaze our pieces, we'll put them in the kiln and they'll be ready to take home tomorrow.

"How did you do that?" I ask. Connor made a beautiful vase. It's tall, which is really hard to do on the wheel. The one time I tried making something half that tall it ended up collapsing in a heap.

"Patience," he says, "and practice."

"You sound like my mom."

"Your mom must be a very intelligent woman."

"More like annoying because she's always right." I start glazing my mug.

"Did I *say* you could sit here?" Ryan growls at Sophie over at the next table. Sophie looks around for another space. There aren't any left.

"You can sit here," I tell her.

Sophie looks at me with so much gratitude that my throat tightens up. I hate how Ryan picks on her. Ryan is one of those people who senses weakness, then attacks. Anytime the two of them have a class together, it's like his personal mission to humiliate her in front of everyone. She's not the only one he hates. Ryan and his stupid prepped-out friends pick on anyone who doesn't fit their warped standards, like kids who are geeky or overweight. Sophie happens to be both.

Ryan also hates Blake something severe. I can't figure out why. Blake lays low and tries so hard to blend in. But every time Ryan passes Blake in the hall, he gives Blake the nastiest looks.

Last year, Ryan ripped up Blake's English essay for no reason. Blake was just sitting there in class, waiting for the teacher to come in and collect everyone's essays. Ryan went over to Blake's desk, snatched up his essay, and ripped it to shreds. It was fifteen pages (fifteen *real* pages, not the bootleg ones with huge fonts and ridiculous margins) and worth most of his grade for the marking period. A bunch of kids saw Ryan do it, but no one told on him. Ryan got away with it. Blake got a zero. Blake was going to hand in the pile of shreds and explain what happened, but he decided to take the zero, as much as it killed him to hurt his grade like that. I think Blake had a feeling where Ryan's hatred was coming from. The last thing Blake wanted to do was push Ryan over the edge.

"Thanks, Lani," Sophie says. She puts her bowl on the table next to my mug.

"No problem," I tell her. "Ryan is a dumbass."

I glare at Ryan. He makes kissy lips back.

Dumbass.

Some kids are watching as Sophie swings her leg over the bench. I'm not even sure if she can fit into the space between me and the hostile sophomore girl on Sophie's other side, but I'm really hoping she can. I'm already scrunched over as far as I can go, teetering on the edge.

Sophie manages to squeeze in between us. The girl on her other side makes an annoyed tooth-sucking sound.

"I like your bowl," I say.

"Thanks." Sophie holds it up. "It's for my sister. She's in college."

"Sweet."

We all zone out in a glazing daze.

When I eventually look up, Ryan's leering at me. I refuse to let him provoke me. I just don't believe in putting more hatred out into the world when someone's directing bad energy at you. I think your fate gets affected by energy, and too much negative energy can be detrimental to your fate.

Example. You ask the Energy for a sign that everything's going to be okay, then you look up and there's some graffiti on the wall that says OK. Those kinds of messages are harder to read when you're all twarked up in a big snit ball of negativity.

I ignore Ryan. It bothers me so much that he makes other people's lives miserable. I think the purpose of life is to help make the world a better place, not to make things worse for everyone. I wonder what it would take for him to get a clue. It's so tragic to think that he'll be like this for the rest of his life.

Sophie gapes at Connor's vase. "Your vase is so tall!"

"Thanks."

"How'd you do that?"

"Patience," I inform her, "and practice."

"Gee, Lani," Connor goes. "That's right. How did you know?"

"Oh, just a wild guess."

He smirks at me. I smirk back.

"Thanks for letting me sit with you guys," Sophie says.

"You don't need an invitation," Connor says. "You can sit with us anytime."

I'm not worried about Connor's karma at all. I hope my karma's as good as his. If I'm destined for any kind of greatness, I don't want to end up damaging my fate.

7

I can't swim.

I know what you're thinking. You're like, *How can you be almost seventeen and not know how to swim?* The thing is, no one ever taught me. When I was little, I never went to camp or to the pool in the summer or anywhere else you would normally learn how to swim. My parents never forced me to be interested and it just never occurred to me to go out and learn.

Until now. We're having a family reunion in Hawaii the summer after graduation (I'm one-fourth Hawaiian on my mom's side). I really want to swim in the ocean while I'm there. I love tropical fish. I have a big aquarium in my room with neons and rainbows and two angelfish. My French angelfish is Wallace, and my queen angelfish is Gromit. She's the most gorgeous queen angelfish ever. She also happens to be my favorite. I know you're not supposed to play favorites with your pets, but I don't think the other fish can tell.

It would be awesome to swim with more tropical fish like mine. I hate being unskilled about something so basic that everyone else can do. So I'm taking a swimming class.

In a lot of ways, I'm a water person. Water is an earth element, so it goes with my Taurus tendencies. If I feel really tired, taking a shower is this totally refreshing, therapeutic experience for me. My bathroom is all set up like a spa. I have tons of shower gels and bath bubbles and I'm into aromatherapy, especially ylang-ylang and lavender and lily of the valley. I even like having wet hair fresh from the shower, especially in the summer.

So I'm all about the water. It's just that I'm scared of water when it comes in the form of a lake or an ocean. Or a pond. Or a pool.

I'm terrified of drowning.

Drowning has to be the scariest way to die. Ever since the accident, I've had these nightmares about sinking deeper and deeper underwater, my lungs straining beyond belief. I'm hoping that after I learn how to swim, those nightmares will go away.

My swimming class is every Wednesday after school at the rec center. The only things I've learned how to do so far are to tread water and doggy-paddle. A lopsided, damaged sort of doggy-paddle. I'm the oldest kid in my class. By a lot. Even the first graders can doggy-paddle better than me.

We're supposed to be doing drills with our buddies. My buddy is actually the instructor's assistant, so he already knows how to swim. Everyone else is paired up with another kid their age. For this drill, I have to stretch my arms out and kick my legs straight back. Except I can't. As soon as my feet leave the pool floor, I feel like I'm going to sink and I spaz out.

I hate being so scared. I want to experience that awesome feeling of slicing through smooth water, the way I imagine it feels to other people when I watch them swim. It just seems like I'm never going to get there.

My buddy disagrees.

"You got this," he says. "It's all you."

He holds his hands out for me to lie on. I press my stomach against them and stretch my arms out in front of me. Then I lift my feet up.

Can't. Do. This.

My feet frantically scrabble for the pool floor. I stand there with my heart pounding. I can't even look at him, I'm so ashamed. It's not that I think he'll let me drown. I know he won't. It's just that I might be safe in this pool, but who's going to save me when I'm swimming by myself in the ocean, out there where anything can happen?

8

I'm all frustrated about what happened in swimming yesterday. Why don't I just admit that I'm never going to learn how to swim? Forget diving and all that fancy stuff. Never going to happen. I'm obviously destined to drown in some freak boating accident.

I should just accept my fate and call it a life.

We have a new salad bar in the cafeteria. Which should be good news. Except that it's seriously lame. Idiots are throwing stuff in. The lettuce looks like it's been sitting there for a really long time. Even the carrot shreds are trying to jump ship. So I'm avoiding the salad bar, sliding my tray along the railing. I frown at the lunch selection. I've narrowed my choices down to two: bad or worse.

Someone comes up behind me and bumps their tray into mine. I spin around, annoyed. Then I realize it's Jason.

He's like, "Hey."

"Oh! I didn't know it was you."

"Are you okay?"

"Yeah. Or. Maybe not."

"Want to talk about it?"

"Not especially."

"That's cool."

We push our trays forward.

"So who do you sit with?" he says.

"Um . . ." I glance over at my table. "Some friends from One World."

"Oh, nice."

We push our trays some more.

"We have a variety of delectable selections this afternoon." Jason makes a sweeping gesture over the food case. "Appetizers include suspicious-looking potato things, an array of crumbly apple slices, and some green stuff over there."

"Sounds delicious."

"Absolutely. Moving on to the main course selections . . . uh . . . yeah, I don't know what any of that is. But there's some questionable Jell-O-like substance for dessert, which could be a plus."

"Yay."

"That's exactly what I said when I saw it."

Five minutes ago I felt horrible. I didn't want to talk to

anybody. Now I'm laughing like nothing was ever wrong.

When we get to the end of the line, Jason takes my lunch card. "It's on me." He hands our cards to the cashier. She swipes them, less than impressed.

"Big spender," I tell him.

"I know, right?"

And then we're just there with our trays.

"Anyway," Jason goes.

"Well, see you later," I say.

"Yeah."

I have this giddy, nervous feeling. I sit down at my table.

"Hey, Lani," Danielle says. "Did you get my note?"

"Yeah. It was hilarious." Danielle knows I've been in a skank mood all day. Sometimes when she wants to cheer me up, she writes me funny notes and slips them in my locker. They usually have parts of conversations she overheard that she knows I'd like. This one was about how some senior smokes so much pot that he only has like six brain cells left. And how he's clinging to his six brain cells.

I can't eat anything.

Danielle's like, "Can you even brush your teeth with only six brain cells left?"

"I don't think you can recognize your toothbrush," I say. I'm not really paying attention, though. I keep looking over at Jason's table. He's laughing with the Golden Kids every time I look.

"Oh, I finally got Good to Go on board." Danielle and I have been working on an initiative to get delis and fast-food places to stop automatically dumping a pile of napkins and stuff in every to-go bag. We've already gotten a few places to agree to ask if you want anything extra.

"That's awesome," I say.

"Yeah, but we still have a lot of places to contact."

When lunch is almost over, I get up to throw out my garbage. Jason gets up with his tray at the same exact time.

I'm separating my regular garbage from the things to recycle, but Jason doesn't do that. He just tosses everything into the garbage can.

I go, "Uh, excuse me?"

"Hi."

"What are you doing?"

"Throwing out my garbage. Unless, do you want it, or—"

"Ring ring! Clue phone!"

Jason stares at me.

"The clue phone is ringing! It's for you!"

"Oh, right. Uh . . . hello?"

"Hi. Is Jason there?"

"Speaking."

"Are you aware that you're supposed to put your empty water bottle in the blue recycling bin?"

"This one?" Jason points to the bin. "Oh, sorry, I forgot you can't see me. I'm currently pointing to the blue recycling bin."

"You mean the one marked bottles and cans?"

"That would be the one, yes."

I wait.

"So I guess I should take my water bottle out of the trash," he concludes.

"That would be a start."

Jason peers into the gross garbage can. "It has noodles on it."

"Do you want to be responsible for completely destroying the only planet you can possibly live on?"

Jason crinkles up his nose. He slowly extends his arm down into the garbage can. He picks up the bottle and shakes some noodles off.

"See?" I go. "That wasn't so bad, was it?"

"It kind of was."

"How can you not recycle?"

"Oh, *I* recycle."

"Yeah? Then what about that bottle?"

"Okay. See I recycle? But just not every single thing every single time."

"Did you know that landfills produce thirty-six percent of all methane emissions?"

"I did not know that."

"And that methane is a major greenhouse gas? Twenty times more powerful than carbon dioxide?"

"That I knew."

"So when you throw something in the garbage that could have been recycled and it becomes part of the landfill mass, you're contributing to human-forced global warming and, ultimately, environmental demise."

Jason considers this. "Tell you what. You convince me that recycling this bottle would make that much of a difference, and I'll promise to recycle everything recyclable for the rest of the year."

"The rest of the *school* year?"

"Yup."

"But that's only two more months."

"Exactly!" And then he smiles like he just solved the global-warming problem all by himself.

"How about for the rest of your life?"

"Whoa. Isn't that a little extreme?"

"Less extreme than destroying the Earth."

"Hmm. Okay. You're on."

"Great." I put my tray on the rack and head back to my table.

"Hey!"

I spin around. "Yes?"

"What about convincing me?"

"I'll have it ready for you soon."

"Why can't you just tell me?"

"How lame would that be? No, I'm doing graphs and charts and whatnot. It'll provide a much more compelling argument."

This will be fun. Here's a chance to show Jason what I know. And maybe even change his life.

9

Sometimes Erin and I go into town together. It's this ritual we've had since forever. Our moms used to take turns driving us. Now that Erin drives us, the ritual feels completely different. It used to be like this special treat I'd look forward to. But now we can go anytime we want. I guess you could say the magic is fading.

The things we like to do in town are still the same, though:

- See if Eye's Gallery has any new jewelry (Erin always needs more rings; I like necklaces).
- Get waffle cups at Ben & Jerry's (Cherry Garcia for me; Imagine Whirled Peace for her).
- Check out what's new at the pet store (aquarium toys for me; cat stuff for her).

- Attack the used bookstore (she usually walks out with a stack of books; I'm lucky to find one I like).
- Walk by the psychic's place. When we do this, I pretend I'm not looking in.

The psychic sits at a small, round table near the window. There's a sign hanging in the window that says PSYCHIC: READINGS & FORTUNES. I want to look in and I don't want to look in at the same time, so I usually end up compromising by sneaking looks. I'm sure she knows what I'm doing. Since she's psychic and all.

Sometimes I think life would be so much easier if I knew everything that was going to happen. If the Unknown could be obliterated, I wouldn't have to be so afraid of it. I could finally know what it feels like to be fearless. But the truth could be ugly. What if something horrible is going to happen to me again? I don't know if I'd be able to live with that information.

"Let's go in," I say.

"Where?" Erin says. "There?"

"Yeah. Why not?"

"I already did your reading."

We're not scheduled to learn about palm reading until next month, but Erin's so fascinated by it that she's learned the basics already. She read our palms a while ago. I don't doubt her skills and I don't want to offend her. But this is our chance to confirm everything she said with a professional. Maybe we can even find out more. Erin only learned about palm reading from books, not from actual experience. I think someone who's been reading palms for a long time can see heavier things.

"I know, but wouldn't it be cool for a psychic to do our readings?" I say. "This *is* tarot month. She has cards."

We look in the window. There's a deck of tarot cards and some candles on the table. The mismatched chairs have bright patterns. The psychic isn't sitting at her usual place. Maybe she's in the back, having lunch.

"She's not even there," Erin says.

"We could wait."

"If she's not back in five minutes, we're leaving."

"Deal."

Erin's like, "Ooh, I forgot to tell you! Jason and I are destined to be together."

"Like this is news?"

I've never seen Erin so excited about a boy. Jason is all she ever talks about. When I try talking about something else, somehow the conversation always leads back to him. Everyone at school is saying how Erin and Jason make the cutest couple and aren't they so perfect together and why didn't they start going out a long time ago? The Golden Circle is thrilled. The whole world is pretty much in agreement that they're meant to be.

"I did some new stuff last night," Erin goes. "Remember that numerology thing I showed you where you take the letters of your name and the letters of the name of the boy you like—"

"Yeah?"

"I did it with me and Jason and it shows we're highly compatible. Then I did our star charts and they said how we're each other's missing piece."

"Star charts tell you that?"

"Totally. Well, not directly. You know . . . you have to interpret the results and all, but that was the obvious message."

The psychic suddenly appears. She's all exotic looking, wrapped in layers of flowy fabrics.

"It's like she knew we were here," I whisper.

"Or her break's over."

The psychic smiles when she sees us. She motions for us to come in. I assumed she'd be intimidating. That's part of the reason why I always avoided her gaze when I walked by before. But she's not intimidating at all. She seems friendly.

"So . . . can we go in?" I say.

"Okay, fine. But you're paying."

"Done."

Bells chime when we push the door open. Inside, it's all incense and woven rugs and dried flower arrangements. There's an entire wall covered with a mosaic of mirrors cut into diamond shapes. The diamonds are all different sizes, outlined with every kind of color.

"I'm so glad you're here," the psychic says. She's still not scary. "I'm Coral."

"I'm Lani and this is Erin."

"Please." Coral waves us over to the small table. It's so weird being on the other side of the window. We go over and sit in the two chairs across from hers. "Would both of you like your fortunes read?"

"Yes, please," I say, feeling like I'm four years old and asking for a cookie. "We'd like our palms read."

"I do both palm and tarot readings. Ten dollars for each of you."

I take a mental inventory of my wallet and decide I have enough to pay for both of us, plus get a waffle cup after. "Okay."

Erin says I should go first, so Coral takes her to a waiting room and closes the door behind her. Then she sits across the table from me. She indicates that I should hold my palm out. I stretch my hand across the table to her.

Coral says, "Your heart line is strong. Bold. You will have great loves in your life."

"More than one?" I ask. I wasn't even sure I'd be lucky enough to have one great love.

"Yes." She brushes her fingers over my palm. "Your health line is missing. That means good health. Your life line is long and deep. You will have a long, full life." She looks some more. "You'll be married. With two children."

So crazy! I've always had a feeling that's exactly how my life would turn out.

"Your head and life lines are joined here," Coral continues. "You think more than you act."

Which is so true again. When Erin read my palm, she told me I'd have a happy love life and live for a long time, but Coral is more specific.

"Your head line is deep. You have a good memory. You're logical. You will have good mental abilities later in life."

I want to ask about my overall fate, but it might be a stupid question. It's not like I expect there to be a fate line.

Being psychic, Coral goes, "Do you have a question?"

"Is there . . . a way to know about my fate? Like, overall?"

"The fate line. It's the line of destiny." She bends my fingers back a little. "See this star here? Under your middle finger?"

I nod.

"This means you will find success after ten years of hard work."

It's amazing how you can tell all this stuff about your life just from some lines on your hand. And how everyone's lines are so different. I have a lot of lines on my hands and most of them are deep, but Erin only has a few lines on hers.

"I see a break in the fate line," Coral says. "In this time of your life, fate will present an immense conflict."

"Now?"

"It's hard to tell exactly when something will happen. We can only see parts of a lifetime. But yes, this conflict will be soon."

Coral pushes the deck of tarot cards across the table to me. She tells me to cut the deck once. Then she flips some cards over and arranges them on the table. I'm liking her prediction about a new boy who's going to change my life forever. Her interpretation of the other cards isn't too shocking. Until she flips the last card over.

"You are bonded to another by a tragic event, but will be ripped apart by one more."

I wait for Coral to explain this. She just gathers up the cards.

"Um . . . what does that mean? Exactly?"

Coral says, "Time will tell."

Then she sends me to the waiting room to get Erin. It's her turn now.

10

The annual kite festival is one of the best things about spring. Aside from school ending in less than two months and the weather getting warmer.

The kite festival has rules.

Not that I've ever paid attention to them. I usually just come to see all the amazing kites. Then I'll borrow someone's kite to fly after. This year I came with Erin and Jason. Jason is entering his kite in the competition. He made it himself.

That's one of the rules, according to the brochure I'm reading for the first time ever. The kite you fly in the contest has to be one that you made or that someone else made for you. Lots of people bring their own kites to fly for fun, but unless they're homemade you can't enter them. Another rule is that a kite can't weigh more than five pounds. Some of these kites are so massive that I can't believe they're less than five pounds.

Kites can win these awards:

- Largest kite
- Smallest kite
- Most unusual kite
- Fifty-yard dash
- Highest-angle kite
- Strongest-pulling kite
- Steadiest kite

The park is getting more crowded with contestants and their guests. Everywhere you look, kites in bright colors float in the breeze. It's amazing how elaborate some of them are. There are dragon ones and butterfly ones and ones with lots of spirals. The whole thing is beyond impressive.

I spread a blanket out under a tree. Erin opens her cooler and hands me my water bottle. I always carry a stainless-steel water bottle because I drink a lot of water. I absolutely refuse to drink soda. Soda causes gut rot. I'm not having that.

Jason's across the grass, looking for us. I wave to him. He smiles when he sees us and comes over. He has the contestant number 15 pinned to his shirt.

"Bummer that I'm in the adult division," Jason goes. The brochure said that the adult division is sixteen and over. "I would have schooled those kids."

"Everyone knows about your advanced kite skills," Erin says.

"That's why they put you with the adults. The kids were way too scared." She jumps up and wraps her arms around Jason. He hugs her back.

Jason's kite looks like a giant loop with all these cool colors and shapes on it. I'd love to know how he made it.

"How did you decide what shape to make your kite?" I ask.

"Aerodynamics, mainly. And a long, boring story I won't be telling here."

"Hey," Erin says. "You never told me that story."

"That would be because it's long and boring."

I'm like, "So which competitions are you entering?"

"I'm going for the fifty-yard dash and highest-angle kite."

"Oh." I nod like I know what *highest-angle kite* means. The brochure didn't really say.

Jason carefully puts his kite down on the grass. Then he opens the cooler and digs around. "Is there any grape soda?"

"Sorry," Erin says. "They didn't have any."

He takes out a water instead. Erin's putting on sunblock, even though it's only April and not that hot out. We learned about the importance of sunblock the hard way when we came to this last year. It was a day just like this—cool and partially cloudy. Erin didn't even think about bringing sunblock. The next day at school, her arms were so red everyone was calling her Lobster Arms. She was mortified. My skin is naturally darker, kind of like I have a permanent tan. So you couldn't really tell that I was also a little sunburned.

Jason sits with us on the blanket.

I go, "So what does 'highest-angle kite' mean, exactly?"

"It's like if you're standing in one spot? How close to being above your head the kite gets."

"Oh! Cool."

"So for that one, we all stand in a line and the judges look at the angle the kite is making with the horizon."

"I remember the fifty-yard dash from last year," Erin says. "You have to keep the kite airborne for the whole run, right?"

"Exactly." Jason looks at me. "Were you here last year, too?"

"I come every year. I love kites."

"Really?"

"Kites are awesome. I also love hot-air balloons."

"Have you ever been in one?"

"No. But you know how they sometimes come down near Smoke Rise?"

"Dude. I've been there so many times."

"Whenever we saw a hot-air balloon when I was little, I got in the car with my mom and we followed it. Then we'd get out to watch when it looked like it was coming down."

"Your mom sounds cool."

"Hey, Erin!" A boy comes running up to us. He looks like he's in fifth or sixth grade. "I didn't know you were coming!"

"Where else would I be?" Erin bends down to hug the grinning kid. He's so happy to see her, the way kids always get around Erin. She's been a babysitter for like half the town. "Chris," she says, "you know Jason, right?"

"Oh, yeah," Chris goes. "Hey."

"Hey," Jason says. He's not exactly getting a hug from Chris.

"And this is my friend Lani," Erin says. "I'm mentoring Chris," she tells me.

Erin just started mentoring at the middle school with Jason. He's been mentoring since last year and kept telling Erin she'd love it. It was a no-brainer for her. The only reason it took her a while to commit to it was that she had to figure out how to cram it into her schedule. Especially since her schedule increasingly consists of quality time with Jason.

"How's the math going?" Erin asks.

"Nowhere," Chris says. "The math part of my brain doesn't work."

"Yes, it does. I'll help you some more. You'll see."

"I hope you're right."

"So where's your family?" Erin asks.

Chris points to an area jammed with little kids. His mom is simultaneously trying to get a baby to stop crying, keep two little boys from killing each other, and tie a bow in a girl's hair.

"Why don't you go help your mom?" Erin says. "I'll see you Tuesday, right?"

"Yeah!" Chris goes. "Bye, Erin!" Then he runs back to his mom.

"I'm getting a snow cone," Erin goes. "Who wants one?"

"I'm good," Jason says.

I go, "I do."

"Cherry?" Erin asks.

"Of course."

And then it's just us.

Jason scratches his knee. "Are there any apples in there?"

"Umm . . ." I check the cooler. "There's one left."

"Nice. Can I have it?"

"It's mine."

"It's yours?"

"Yeah. I called it like an hour ago. Didn't you hear me?"

"Not really."

"Tough break."

"I'll rock-paper-scissors you for it."

"You're on."

We get our fists ready. Jason goes, "Rock paper scissors say *shoot*!" I throw a scissors and he throws a paper.

"Ooh," I say. "Another tough break."

"Two out of three."

"You didn't say that before."

"I'm saying it now."

"It doesn't count now. You have to say it before."

"Says who?"

"Those are the rules. Don't you know the rules?"

"Oh," Jason says, "I *am* the rules."

We drink our water.

"When's your birthday?" I go.

"October first."

Of course Jason's a Libra. He's charming, agreeable, easy-going, and idealistic. All classic Libra characteristics. I was hoping he'd be a sign that's compatible with Taurus and incompatible with Leo. This is really interesting. He's actually not compatible with either one of us.

Okay, what am I even thinking? We're just friends. I'm happy for Erin. Life is good.

"Why?" Jason says.

"I was just wondering. My birthday's coming up, so . . ."

Sunlight hits Jason's eyes in a way that makes it hard to look at him. He has these amazing green-blue eyes.

Must. Stop. Looking.

Jason's like, "Where's Blake?"

"He's not as fascinated by kites as I am."

Jason does this contemplative nodding thing I've noticed before. Kind of like, *Someone's not fascinated with kites. Wild.* "So . . . he's at home, or . . . ?"

"I guess. I don't know."

Jason drinks his water. "It's cool how you're not one of those couples that has to do everything together. You know?"

Oh my god. Jason thinks Blake is my *boyfriend*? Where did he get that?

"Blake's not my boyfriend," I say.

"He's not?"

"No." I want to explain. But of course I can't.

"Oh." Jason smiles a little. He drinks more water to hide it.

One thing I've learned about boys? Is that when they ask if you have a boyfriend (or they say that you have one, so you either end up confirming that you do or you don't), it means they're interested in you and they're trying to find out if you're available. There's no way Jason is interested in me, though. He likes Erin. Erin and I are so different that he couldn't possibly like us both. Plus, if he liked me instead, he would have asked me out.

Right?

11

I've been sitting with Jason at lunch all week, ever since the kite festival. Sitting together shouldn't be a big deal. People should be able to sit wherever they want.

Of course, it's not that simple.

My friends are acting like I insulted them. The Golden Circle keeps glaring at us. Bianca seems particularly aggravated. She blatantly stares at us as if it's acceptable behavior. Which just makes me more determined to do what I want. I refuse to let them control me with their negativity.

Over at the Golden Table, Greg gets up. He smiles at us. He waves.

Jason ignores him.

"Greg's waving at you," I say.

"No, he's not."

"Um, I think he is."

"That's not a real wave. It's a sarcastic wave."

"How can you tell?"

"He's been giving me a hard time about switching tables. You'd think it was a federal offense or something."

"My friends don't like it, either. I think they're insulted. But it's not like we're not friends anymore! I'm just sitting somewhere else. Why does it have to be a monumental deal?"

There's no way I can be in here with Jason and not want to sit with him. I'm hoping he feels the same way, because he's the one who asked if I'd sit with him. But it's not like I could just go over and sit with him at the Golden Table. And he wasn't about to come over to my table and sit with a bunch of girls he never talks to. So we had to stake out new territory.

Jason's like, "This sucks."

"I know," I say. "I can't wait for next year." Seniors get to leave campus for lunch. They can go home or over to the lunch counter or the pizza place. We're stuck in cafeteria hell for the rest of the year. "It's so unfair. Look how nice it is out!"

"This blows."

"I thought it sucked."

"Dude, it's doing both. It's out of control."

"I am *so* going to the lunch counter next year." The lunch counter is this old-school sandwich place that's been around for, like, a hundred years. You go in and it's just this long counter you sit at on one of these retro diner stools. Their sandwiches are really good and cheap. It's fun to pretend you're stuck in 1960-whatever for a little while.

Bianca is staring at us. Again.

I block out her negative vibes.

Jason's like, "Here's something." He takes out a notebook. His notebook is actually pretty neat for a boy's. There aren't any pages sticking out, all crumpled.

"Nice notebook," I tell him.

"Really?"

"Yeah."

"Why?"

"It's not falling apart."

"Oh! That. I try to apply organizational notebook skills whenever possible." Jason rips a page out. Some fringies fly out of the spiral part. "Do you like codes?"

"Absolutely."

"Good answer."

"What do you mean by codes?"

Jason laughs. "I like to make up codes so no one can figure out what I'm writing."

"Like for passing secret notes and stuff?"

"Exactly."

"I love that!" I don't know how he does it, but Jason always comes up with these fun, bizarre activities. So far during our week of sitting together, he's shown me how to:

- Watch a conversation from across the room and invent dialogue for it.
- Use grapes and string cheese as an abacus.

- Apply *Farmer's Almanac* weather forecasts to predict teachers' moods.

I glance at my usual table. Danielle is talking with some other kids from One World, half turned away from me, eating the baby carrots she always brings for lunch. I watch her fidget with her glasses. She always fidgets with her glasses when she's stressed. I wish Danielle would look at me. I'd smile so she'd know I'm not ignoring her or anything. She wasn't exactly understanding about me leaving the table. I had no idea she'd be so sensitive about it. I mean, we still see each other every day. We're still good friends. Just because I'm sitting at a different table doesn't change any of that.

Bianca's still staring. I don't know why the Golden Circle finds us so fascinating. There's zero drama here. Erin knows we sit together. She says it will give me a chance to find out what Jason thinks about her, so she's fine with it. I'm not sure if she's assuming we're just sitting together for a few days as a temporary thing, but the year is almost over so I really don't think it matters.

"So with this one . . ." Jason digs a pencil out of his bag. "The first letter of every word represents one letter in your message. You use periods to separate words. So like—" He writes something on the paper. "Here."

He passes me this:

Heaven inside. To helicopters everywhere riding elephants.

I'm like, "Helicopters can ride elephants?" Clearly, I'm not the most adept code-breaker.

"It doesn't matter what it says," Jason explains. "The sentences don't have to make sense. It's all about the code."

"Okay . . ."

"So what does it say?"

I take his pencil and write the first letter of each word below what he wrote. When I see how easy it was to get "Hi there," I'm embarrassed I wrote anything down.

Jason's handwriting is fascinating. I learned about graphology all the way back in October, but I still remember some things. He has this whole forward, upward slant to his writing. This indicates emotional expressiveness and optimism. I also notice that he uses a lot of pressure when he writes, which means he's intense.

"Sweet," I go. "Did you invent this yourself?"

"Can you believe how brilliant I am?"

"Not really."

"Now you go."

There are some things I really want to tell him. But it's not like I can actually say any of those things. So I just write:

Cucumbers on our level. Can one decide enough?

I pass it over to him. "I wasn't sure if you're allowed to use question marks."

"Oh, you're allowed. If they go with your coded sentence."

"This one goes."

Jason looks at the paper for a minute. "One more." He writes something and passes it over.

Really intense guys have trouble.

"Hey!" I go. "This actually makes sense!" It's so weird how I just analyzed that he's intense and here he is writing about it. Not that I'm going to share that information. I don't want him thinking I'm some creepy girl who goes around analyzing people's writing or anything.

"Yeah. You get bonus points for that."

"So, what kind of trouble are you having?"

"How do you know it's referring to me?"

"Because you're an intense guy."

"Ah, but am I a *really* intense guy?"

"I can't tell yet."

"This code works on a few different levels. Like every time I say *right*, it could actually mean this."

"Handy." I can already tell that Jason is really intense. He gets things average boys don't. He seems more aware than other people. You can see it in his eyes. I can definitely see it when he looks at me. Especially when the color of his eyes changes. Sometimes we'll be talking or laughing and suddenly it's like a switch flips and he gets all serious. That's when his eyes change from their normal tropical ocean green-blue to a much darker green.

When that happens, it's definitely intense.

"Does every intense guy have trouble?" I ask.

"Only when they're in difficult situations."

"Like what?"

Jason gets his serious look. His eyes go dark green.

I press my fingers against my tourmalinated quartz. It hangs from a silver chain I always have on, even if I'm wearing other necklaces. Tourmalinated quartz has balancing powers. It grounds me when I'm feeling unstable.

Fricking busted tourmalinated quartz.

I go, "You mean . . . like when your pizza gets cold and you don't want it anymore?"

Jason looks down at his cold slice of pizza.

"Right," he says. "That's exactly what I mean."

We both know it's not.

Or maybe I'm the only one feeling these things. Jason made his choice. I'm not it. So I need to just accept that being friends with him is going to be hard, but I'd rather be friends than nothing at all.

12

Today's my birthday. It's really cool how astrology totally determines who you are. Like when I learned about birth charts, here's what I found out about my inherent attributes:

may 5

- Revolutionary
- multitalented
- Clever
- Progressive
- Original

I also discovered that my moon sign is Aquarius. I think my moon-sign characteristics are more accurate:

moon in Aquarius

- Attraction to astrology
- Supports great causes
- Strong ideals
- True humanitarianism
- Eccentric interests

The moon and the stars know us. More proof that everything is connected.

Erin and Blake are coming over tonight. Erin wanted to bring Jason, so he's coming, too. I didn't invite anyone else. I hate big parties if they're for me. I was thinking about inviting Danielle, but when I mentioned it to Erin, she sort of convinced me not to.

I was like, "I might invite Danielle."

Erin went, "Oh," in that way where someone's partially repulsed by something.

"What?" I said.

"Nothing. It's just . . . do you think that's the best idea? I mean, she doesn't really know us."

"She knows me." Erin has issues with Danielle. It bothers her that Danielle and I became good friends after I broke away from the Golden Circle. If Erin had her way, nothing would have changed. *Danielle* and *fun* aren't exactly synonymous in Erin's mind. They've never hung out, which is fine by Erin.

"No offense," Erin went, "but it'd be way better if it was just the four of us. You're the only one she knows. Don't you think she'd feel left out?"

Erin had a point. Inviting Danielle might be awkward for her.

So I decided not to invite Danielle. When she asked what I was doing for my birthday, I told her I just wanted to chill alone because I really needed some Me Time. I hated lying to her, but I had no idea what else to say.

One World threw me a party during our meeting yesterday. Danielle even made a cake. No one was mad about my lunch table switch. Actually, things only feel weird with Danielle at lunch. When we hang out like we usually do, everything seems the same as always. Mom did a huge birthday breakfast spread this morning. As part of their gift, my parents are spending the night in the city so we can have the house to ourselves. It seems more like a gift for them, but whatever. We're going to order in and watch movies.

I've been thinking about what happened at lunch the other day with the note code. I've decided it was nothing. Jason does not like me. I cannot like him.

It's obviously nothing.

Blake doesn't agree.

"She's bringing him *here*?" Blake thinks I'm mental for hanging out with Jason while Erin's in the same room. He couldn't believe that Erin didn't figure out that Jason likes me when we were at the kite festival. I tried to explain that the reason Erin didn't figure it out is because there's nothing *to* figure out. He's convinced I'm in denial. And not just about Jason liking me. Blake thinks I like him back.

"What's the big deal?" I go.

"The big *deal*? Seriously?"

I'm digging through the kitchen drawer with all the miscellaneous stuff, trying to find the take-out menus. We hardly ever use them since my mom cooks almost every night.

Blake goes, "It's obvious he likes you—"

"Can you *not*?" I interrupt.

"Can I finish?"

I go back to digging through the drawer.

"As I was saying," Blake continues, "it's obvious he likes you. And it's obvious you like him."

"Why do you keep saying that?"

"Why do you keep denying it?"

I stop digging.

Blake goes, "You know how some people's feelings are written all over their faces?"

"Yeah?"

"You should see yourself when he's around. It's like you guys had this instant connection."

"Just because two people connect doesn't mean they like each other."

"No. But you do."

"If it's so obvious, then how come Erin hasn't said anything?"

"Please, you know how that one is. She's wrapped up in her own world. True, it's a fabulous world, but she pretty much just sees what she wants to see."

It was one thing for Blake to joke about the way Jason looked at me when we all went out for pizza. It's a whole other thing for him to mean it. He's probably just picking up on my vibes and projecting them onto Jason. He also seems to be confusing having things in common with attraction. They're two totally different things.

"Right?" Blake goes.

"I'm neither confirming nor denying my own feelings, but trust me: Jason likes Erin. That's why he's going out with her."

There are so many reasons why Jason can't like me. But I still can't stop thinking about my palm and tarot readings. How I'll have more than one great love in my life. How my fate line shows that an immense conflict will happen soon.

How something might rip Erin and me apart.

The doorbell rings.

I go, "Can I put my head in this drawer and slam it now?"

"Not now. You have company."

"Okay." I take a deep breath. "I can do this. It's not that serious."

"Not yet," Blake mumbles.

"What?"

"Get the door, girl. One step at a time."

"Ha-ha." I've totally converted Blake on the horoscope front. Now we read our weekly horoscopes together. This week, my horoscope said that I'd be faced with a great challenge and the best way to approach it would be one step at a time.

Somehow, I manage to open the door. And smile at the enormous bunch of balloons Erin has for me. And act like my normal self (or at least what I think my normal self acts like). But I can't stop wondering why I didn't deny it when Blake said I like Jason. I should have just told him he's wrong. Then everything would be fine.

After dinner, two movies, cake, and a hysterical game of Twister, Jason and I are out on the back porch sitting on the swing while Erin and Blake are inside playing more Twister. I don't know how we split up into pairs like this. Maybe Blake had something to do with it. I was laughing so hard playing that I almost hacked up a lung. So I said I was going to take a break and Jason said he'd come with me and Blake challenged Erin to another game and here we are.

My back porch is elevated over the lake. When you're on the porch, it looks like you're floating above the water. It's really peaceful. We can hear "Transatlanticism" playing through the open window. It's one of the songs on my desert-island CD pick. Death Cab is made of awesome.

"I like it out here," Jason says.

"Me, too."

"You can see defunct tracks right through those trees over there."

"What?"

"Old train tracks. Some parts of the rail line aren't used anymore, but the tracks are still there. The train used to go right along that side of the lake."

"How long ago was that?"

"Don't know. Like, fifty years ago?"

"How do you know all this?"

"My grandpa was a train conductor. We used to go for walks when I was little, all up and down these tracks. He showed me tons of secret places they go."

"That's so cool."

A warm breeze blows over the lake. These May nights are the best. The air is really soft. By July, it's so hot and humid out that the suffocating air practically crushes you the second you leave the house.

"I still walk them," Jason says. "The tracks."

"Yeah?"

"Yeah. My grandpa used to say that any problem I had could be worked out by walking the tracks. He said I could find all the answers out there."

How perfect would that be? I could use that kind of magic right about now.

"Do you think it's true?" I ask.

"It works for me. Whenever I can't get something out of my head, I walk the tracks. Everything just sort of clears away."

"I used to have a journal. The same thing would happen with me. As soon as I wrote about my problems, it was like they weren't so bad anymore."

"Exactly. Once you put it all out there, you're free."

Jason gets me. He even gets stuff I didn't know I was trying to say.

He goes, "Maybe you can come with me sometime."

"Where?"

"For a walk."

"Okay. I mean, maybe. Not that I don't want to. It's—that sounds cool. I'm just not sure if . . . whatever. Walks are good."

Walks are good? Could I *be* a bigger spaz? What's the big deal about walking? Not that Jason and I will be walking anywhere now. Now that he knows what a complete and total freak I am.

"Do you still have a journal?" Jason says.

"No. I thought about starting a blog, but that's not really my thing."

"So what's your thing?"

"What do you mean?"

"How do you deal with your problems?"

"Oh." I take a mental inventory of the things I do to feel better. Use my favorite bath bubbles. Do some more fate research. Plant trees. Somehow, none of my usual techniques has been all that effective lately. "I guess I don't, really. Deal with them, I mean."

It's so weird about Jason and the train tracks. When I was little, I was always fascinated by them. Where they were going. What they had seen. I wondered if anyone else was noticing them the way I was. There's something about the train tracks that made me feel like I was in the center of everything, like I could go anywhere. The world felt so full of possibility. So I think it's wild that this whole time, there was someone else out there who felt the same way.

And now he's here.

"Everyone has their coping tricks," Jason says. "Let's see. Do you . . . get mad at the world and punch holes in the wall?"

"No."

"No? Do you . . . eat ice cream and watch chick flicks?"

"No."

"Are you sure?"

"Yes."

"Are you ticklish?"

"No!" I yell. Because I am so ticklish it's not even funny.

"Let's make sure." Jason tickles my side.

"Stop!" I laugh-scream. "Stop it!"

The porch door slides open.

"Hey," Erin says.

Jason stops tickling me.

I stop laughing.

"Oh, hey," he says. "We were just . . . talking."

"About what?"

I can't really remember what we were talking about. Something about journals and train tracks and . . . How did that turn into all the tickling?

Erin looks at me.

I go, "Um. Just . . . you know . . . random stuff . . ."

"How's Twister?" Jason says.

"Over."

Blake swoops up behind Erin. He lifts her up and carries her out to the porch.

"Put me down!" she squeals.

"Not until you admit that I am the reigning Twister champion of all time that was and all time left to come."

"Fine."

"That doesn't sound convincing!" Blake lifts her higher.

"Okay, okay! You rule!"

"Thank you." Blake puts Erin down.

"But you *so* cheated on left-hand yellow!" Erin yells. Then she runs off the porch shrieking with Blake chasing her. He catches her and carries her back.

"It's getting late," Erin tells Jason. "I should go." She sneaks a quick look at me. The sparkle in her eye says, *Fill me in on what he said later?*

I give her a little nod. I wish I had something good to tell her.

"Yeah, okay." Jason gets up.

I stay on the swing. I'm surprised at how much I don't want him to leave.

"So . . ." Jason goes. "Happy birthday. Thanks for having us over. It was fun."

"Of course. Anytime."

Anytime? Why did I say that? It sounds like an invitation to come over and make out or something.

Blake sits on the swing next to me after letting them out. I'm in a total daze. I can't even get up.

We listen to Jason's Jeep pulling out of the driveway.

"How's it going?" Blake says.

"I wish I knew."

"Are you okay?"

"Yeah."

"What happened out here?"

"Nothing."

I'm sure that's exactly how it felt to Jason. Like nothing happened. I just wish that to me, it didn't feel like something.

13

We're doing pointillism in art. It's a method of painting where the image you're creating consists of all these tiny dots. The cool thing is that you can only see the dots up close. When you look at the painting from far away, it just looks like a regular painting. Pointillism is really hard because it takes forever to make all the little dots. And getting the right colors in the right places is key. If your colors are corroded in one little section, it ruins the whole painting.

Naturally, Connor rocks at pointillism.

"You're so good at everything," I tell him. "I suck at this."

"No you don't," he says. He's just being nice. I'm trying to paint an underwater ocean scene. It's just not working. My queen angelfish is supposed to have these bright yellow eyes and electric-blue stripes along the edge of her fin. Instead, it looks like I'm trying to paint a fried egg with some blue bacon. Maybe I can pass it off as postmodern.

"Are you sure I don't suck?" I ask.

"Positive."

"Then what's this supposed to be?" I slide my paper across the table to Connor.

He turns the paper around and barely looks at it before sliding it back. He goes, "A fish."

"How did you do that?"

"You're not as bad as you think. It looks good."

"Really?"

"Yes."

People are always telling me that I'm too hard on myself. That's part of being a Taurus. I can be so stubborn about making things perfect that I don't stop to notice they're already good enough.

"What do you think of mine?" Sophie asks me. She's been sitting with me and Connor since that day Ryan harassed her. She doesn't really say much.

"It's good!" I say.

"Thanks." She grins at the table.

Sophie and Connor are so much better at this. I've been blending red and blue together for ten minutes and I still can't get the exact shade of purple I want.

"Maybe it doesn't exist," I tell myself. But I say it out loud.

"What?" Connor says.

"This color I'm trying to make. Maybe it's not an actual color."

"Kind of lost me there."

"I mean, have all the colors been invented already? Or are there some new colors that don't exist yet?"

"Still lost."

"Like . . . how are colors . . . made?"

"How are they *made*?"

"Yeah."

"From pigment combinations."

"Well, where do pigments come from?"

"I think they're just naturally occurring."

"Naturally occurring in what?"

"Um . . ."

I hate when questions like this get stuck in my head. They bother me until I can find an answer. The annoying thing is that these kinds of questions usually don't have definite answers. Like with the whole fate thing. Do we have control over our fate, or will our lives turn out the same way no matter what we do? This is the one question I wish I could know the answer to more than any others. But I'll probably never know.

Ms. Sheptock lets us out early. This happens sometimes when she has to set up complicated project materials for the advanced art class she has next. I go to get a drink of water near the locker room. I wonder if Danielle's around. She has gym now.

Just when I'm about to leave, Danielle comes out of the gym with a group of girls. They pass by in a cloud of cherry lip gloss and Secret deodorant, disappearing into the locker room.

"Hey," she goes. "You got out early from art again?"

"Just in time. I was two seconds away from ripping my pointillism fiasco to shreds."

"You're too hard on yourself."

"Only when it's true."

"So . . . I've been meaning to ask you something."

"What?"

Danielle looks behind her, toward the locker room. No one's around.

"I just . . ." She gets really quiet. "I was wondering if . . . there's anything going on with you and Jason."

"What? No! Why would you think that?"

"Because you sit with him every day at lunch."

"I thought you weren't mad about that. I told you, it's—"

"I'm not mad. I just meant . . . I see the way you are with him."

This is tricky. I could ask exactly what she means by that. Of course I want to know. But then we'll be talking about it. It's better to not go there.

"We're just friends," I say. "You know he's with Erin."

"I know."

"We have this connection, is all."

I can tell that Danielle doesn't believe me. We're close. She knows me. So because we're close and she knows me, she's letting it go. That's how you know you have a good friend. When they spare you from a conversation you don't want to have.

When I head to English in a direction that will probably make me late, it's not a conscious decision. Something is making me walk a different way than I normally would when there's no reason I should. You know how you're so used to having the same routine every day that sometimes you're not even aware of how you got from point A to point B? Like, all of a sudden I'll be somewhere that I totally don't remember walking to. I'm used to sort of tuning out like that in between classes. But right now I just have this really strong feeling that I should go down a different hall. So I do.

And there's Jason. Right around the corner.

"Hey," he says. "I never see you before fourth."

"Well . . . here I am."

"Nice. What do you have now?"

"Um. English."

"Do you have Mrs. DeFranco?"

"No, Ms. Martin."

"I hear she's decent."

"Yeah, I like her."

The bell rings.

Jason says, "See you at lunch?"

"Yeah."

We both go to leave at the same time. I bump right into Jason. Or he bumps into me. It's hard to tell.

"Oh!" I go. "Sorry!"

"No, it's my fault. I'm still learning how this whole look-where-you're-going thing works."

We try to walk our separate ways without bumping into each other again. We both move to the same side, then the other side.

"Whoa," Jason says. "Maybe one of us should let the other go first."

"I'm not moving."

"Walking away now."

Jason finally manages to leave.

Kids go to their classrooms. I just stand there, processing it all. What made me walk this way, knowing it would make me late for class? Was the Energy controlling my fate? Or was I controlling my own fate?

14

Today is one of those typical spring Sundays. Mom is working in the garden, planting sunflower seeds. Dad's in his recliner with a new crossword-puzzle book. Erin's over. We're watching a movie in my room. It's the same scenario we've all played out tons of times before. Except today is different.

Today I feel guilty.

Erin doesn't care that Jason and I sit together at lunch. She loves that we're friends now. Before that time we all went out for pizza, she was worried that we wouldn't like each other, which would have harshed her excitement over all of us doing stuff together. So she's relieved that Blake approved Jason as worthy and that I like hanging out with him. With all of their staring at us, I don't know if the Golden Circle has said anything to her. Even if they have, it wouldn't occur to Erin to take their gossiping seriously. In Erin's mind, Jason and I only exist in relation to her. She gets like this sometimes—only seeing what she wants. It's a sort of tunnel vision that makes her oblivious.

Erin wants to know what Jason's been saying about her. But Jason never really talks about Erin. Whenever I bring her up, he changes the subject three seconds later. Not that I bring her up as much as I should. Which is why I'm having trouble answering Erin's questions.

"But what did he *say*?" she goes.

"Nothing."

"You asked him if he liked my hair and he didn't say any-thing?" Erin has curly blonde hair. She just started blowing it out straight. I was supposed to ask Jason if he likes Erin's hair better straight or curly. I mean, I did ask him . . . I think. I'm sure I did. I just can't remember what he said.

"No, he said it looks nice," I tell her.

"He likes it better than curly?"

"I think he likes both ways the same."

"Huh. That's weird."

"Why?"

"Guys have strong opinions about how they want girls to look. They usually either like curly hair or straight hair. Not both."

"I guess Jason's more open-minded."

"I know, isn't he awesome?"

"Totally."

We go back to watching *Thirteen*. But I have this thing lately where I can't concentrate on simple activities. Like, I'll be reading a book and my mind will just drift off and twenty minutes later

I'm still on the same page. Or I'll be watching a movie and a whole scene will go by before I realize that I have no idea what anyone said.

"What do you like best about him?" Erin asks.

"Who?"

"Jason!"

"Oh." I really don't think I'm the best person to ask. Not because I don't have an answer. More like because I have too many answers. "Um . . . he's funny."

"*So* funny."

"And smart."

"*So* smart."

Gromit peers at me from around a bit of coral. I go over to the aquarium and press my finger against the glass. She looks at me curiously. Then, concluding that I am not food, she drifts away.

Erin's like, "Next year's going to be the best."

"Totally."

"We should all do a road trip!"

"Um—"

"We can drive to Arizona and check out that world's largest solar panel you've been dying to see."

"You mean the wind turbine farm at the Solar Center?"

"Whatever. It'll be wild! We'll drive in shifts and stay in random motels. And all those rest stops—you *love* diners!"

I have to laugh at Erin's excitement. She's all about the fun times. You have to admire her determination to get everyone else on board.

"What else did he say about me?" Erin goes.

"When?"

"Whenever! What does he talk about?"

"Just . . ." I don't know what to say. It's not like I can tell her about the time I showed Jason all those charts and graphs to convince him to recycle (which he said he would do from now on because he was totally convinced, by the way). Or how he showed me his note code. Because what if he never showed Erin? What if the code is this secret just between us? Erin might be jealous that he showed me something he didn't show her first.

She's all, "Why won't you tell me?"

"There's nothing—"

"Oh my god—did he say something bad about me? Is that why you're not telling?"

"No! There's nothing to tell."

"Swear?"

"Yes. If he says something about you, I will definitely tell you."

"But shouldn't he have said something by now? Don't you guys talk about me?"

"Sometimes. But there's other stuff going on in the world, you know."

"Okay, I'm overreacting. I need to chill."

When you're in the middle of a situation, sometimes it's hard to see how things really are. Erin can't see what I see. She thinks it's her fate to be with Jason, that they're building a strong relationship that will last for a long time, that he feels the same way about her. But I see something different. To me, it seems like Jason is having a good time with Erin without getting too heavy. I don't doubt that he likes her. I just doubt that he likes her as much as she wants him to.

I'm trying to ignore these things I see. They're the kind of truth you can never tell your best friend.

15

I don't know where it comes from. But Jason and I have this connection that's stronger than anything I've ever felt before. We have this way together where everything clicks. It's so easy to be with him. And when I'm not with him, I can't wait to see him again.

He feels like home to me.

The question is, can you just be friends with a soul mate when you want to be so much more?

It's not as if there's one major thing I can point to and say, "Aha! This is why we're soul mates!" It's a lot of little things, all together. Things that have no real meaning to anyone else but us.

This one time when Jason got coffee from the vending machine, there was something really familiar about the way he drank it. It was like I was watching myself drink coffee because I would do it the same exact way. Not that I ever realized how I drink coffee until he showed me.

Or a few days ago at lunch, when we suddenly started talking in abbreve. When you talk in abbreve, you can't just abbreviate any words whatever way you want. There are rules. The weird thing is, I know the rules without ever having learned them. It would be impossible for me to explain these rules to anyone else. But somehow, Jason already knew them.

I was complaining about my grade on a history paper, and Jason went, "That's ridic."

"Where'd you get that?" I said.

"What?"

"Ridic."

"Isn't it common sense?"

"I don't think so."

"Oh. Well, I guess I have special abbreve talents then."

"You know it's abbreve!"

"Who doesn't know that?"

"Everyone! I thought I made it up."

"I thought *I* made it up."

I have no idea how he knows these things. Like just now, we both scraped off some icing from our pieces of cake at the same time. Then we tapped our forks together and both went, "Cheers." I thought I was the only one who did cheers! Jason has been here all along, with all of these same ways of being, and I never even knew it.

Bianca gets up from the Golden Table. She looks over at us.

When Bianca looks at us, it's not like when other people look. Other people look away when you look back at them. Other people have some sort of grasp on boundaries.

Bianca is not other people.

I already know she's coming over. She's all about the gossip. Even if there's no gossip, she'll make some up anyway. It's so tragic. She wasn't this bad back when we were sort of friends. I don't know how Erin can still deal with her.

"Hey, you guys," Bianca says. She's just standing there like it's the most natural thing in the world for her to come over and talk to us. If we wanted company, we would be sitting at a bigger table with more people at it.

"Hey," Jason says.

Subtext: Why the eff are you bothering us?

"So, Lani," Bianca goes. "I was wondering if Erin's going to camp this summer."

Subtext: I needed an excuse to come over here, so I made up this lame one.

"Why wouldn't she?" I say.

Subtext: You know she's going to camp because she always goes to camp, so why are you asking?

"I thought she was, but my cousin was thinking about going to camp in Vermont so I thought she could talk to Erin about it."

Subtext: Why are you and Jason sitting together?

I'm like, "You could just ask Erin."

Subtext: Lay off.

"I know, I just thought you might know," Bianca says. "Well . . . see ya!"

Jason goes, "What was that?"

"You don't want to know."

Why can't people just leave us alone? I see the way they stare. Or in the hall, when Jason walks with me between classes. I had no idea we were so fascinating.

"This history report is killing me," Jason goes.

"You're still working on that?" Jason's been complaining about his history report forever. He unfortunately got stuck with the one history teacher who enjoys assigning insane amounts of work. "I thought it was due last week."

"No, I have two more days."

"How far are you?"

"Not far enough. And I won't have that much time to work on it later because I have mentoring."

"I wish I could help you."

"What are you doing after school?"

"No, I mean, I wish I could help, but—"

"Dude, I'm talking about mentoring. Want to come with us?"

Jason talks about the kids he mentors sometimes. You can tell that he loves hanging out with those kids just as much as Erin does, trying to help them learn and maybe even make their lives better. It sounds like the kids really like him, too.

My head's all foggy. "Is it Tuesday?" I go.

"Yeah."

"Sweet, I don't have swimming. And One World's not until Thursday."

"You're on the swim team?"

"No, more like . . . I take a class. At the rec center."

"You take swimming classes?"

"I know, I'm like six years old."

"I could teach you."

"Really?"

"Totally. I lifeguard in the summer."

"I didn't know that."

We eat cake.

Jason goes, "So, you don't have swimming because it's Tuesday—"

"Oh, sorry, um . . . I'm not doing anything."

"Cool, you can come to mentoring."

The middle school is a five-minute walk from here. There's no excuse to not go. Except I don't want Erin to feel like I'm intruding. Mentoring is their thing.

"Wouldn't I be a third wheel?" I ask.

"Impossible."

"Are you allowed to bring someone?"

"I don't see why not."

"Maybe we should ask Erin. Just to make sure it's okay."

"I'm all over it."

Erin was totally cool with me going. So we all walked over after school. The middle school has a huge classroom they use for after-school activities. Desks were set up in pairs and small groups. Erin introduced me to some of the kids she's been working with. They all crowded around her adoringly, yammering about five different things at once.

Jason went to help a group with their science homework, and Erin was talking with a student by the bookshelves. I read *Harriet the Spy* with a sixth grader.

After, Erin decided that we should make certificates for the kids in mentoring who've improved the most. We have an awards ceremony at the end of every year, but the middle school doesn't. So Jason said we could come over to his house to work on some certificates.

Driving over to Jason's, Erin goes, "Did you have fun?"

"Tons. It's so cool that you guys mentor."

"Kids are the future," Erin says. "I have to help make sure it doesn't suck." It's so Erin to want to be a part of everything.

We get to Jason's house right as he's getting out of his Jeep. A cute dog is waiting right inside the doorway. He's small and stocky with short black fur.

He snorts loudly when he sees Jason.

"Hey, Phil," Jason goes. "Wanna meet a new friend?"

Erin has obviously already met Phil. She pets him and makes you're-such-a-cute-dog noises.

"What kind of dog is he?" I ask.

"He's a French bulldog. Very dignified."

Phil has big, wet eyes. He stares at me.

Jason's like, "You can pet him."

I put my hand out for Phil to sniff. He snuffles against my fingers.

"I have construction paper in my room," Jason says. "Come on up." He takes the stairs two at a time, ahead of us. We follow with Phil running up the stairs between us, his short legs working away.

The poster is the first thing I see. It's a special-edition poster of *The Little Prince*. I collect all things *Little Prince*. The fox is my favorite character.

I have that same exact poster in my room. I've had it since I was four.

"I have that same poster," I say.

"No way," Jason says. He's digging through a pile of stuff on his desk.

"I collect *Little Prince* things. I've had it forever."

"I bet I've had mine longer."

"Your poster is the same one?" Erin asks me.

"You know it is. Why didn't you tell me we had the same poster?"

"I never noticed. I thought they were both just *Little Prince* in general."

"You've seen my poster hundreds of times. How can you not know—"

"A Koosh," Jason interrupts.

"Huh?"

"I'll bet you a Koosh that I've had my poster longer than you've had yours."

"Any particular colors?"

"Yes."

"Deal."

We shake on it.

"So?" I say.

"I've had my poster . . ."

"Yeah . . . ?"

". . . since I was four."

"Same here!"

"No way."

"Will you stop saying *no way*?" Erin goes. Then, less harshly: "Where's the construction paper?"

Jason doesn't have just any *Little Prince* poster. He has the *same exact one as me*. And we've had our posters for the *same exact amount of time*. These things don't just happen randomly.

Jason's a kindred spirit who's been in my life this whole time and I didn't even know it. We've gone to school together all these years, but it took us this long to discover the truth. So did fate bring us together, using Erin to connect us? Or would we have found each other anyway?

As if it matters. Because it's not just about us. Which is why I have to ignore all of this. Even though it's obvious that nothing this intense will ever happen to me again.

16

I have the hiccups. They won't go away.

"Those sound serious," Jason says.

He ran into me at my locker after English, so we're walking to lunch together. When we pass Bianca at her locker, she jabs her laser glare at me. I resist the urge to slam her face into the wall.

"They are," I say. "Very serious."

"How long have you had them?"

"Ten minutes. At least."

"I know what you need."

"What?"

"That," Jason says, "will be revealed momentarily."

When we bring our lunches to our table, Jason still won't tell me. My hiccups are getting worse, if that's possible.

"Oh," Jason says, "did you drink this water before your hiccups started?" He holds up his water bottle. It's some weird kind with an iceberg on it.

"What kind of water is that?"

"The refreshing iceberg kind, otherwise known as Crisp Icy Water. You've never tried it?"

"No."

"Okay, then it wasn't the water. This brand has been linked to irreversible hiccup damage. Never drink this kind of water."

"You're drinking it."

"Yeah, but I don't have the hiccups. Also, it doesn't have a good color/shape/taste combo going for it."

"*Hic!*"

"I know, that shocked me when I found out, too. But yeah, it tastes like orange rhombus, so that's no fun."

The scary thing is that I know exactly what he's talking about. You can describe the taste of different kinds of water by color and shape. Like, Poland Spring is a red circle. Why it's a red circle is hard to explain. It just is. I guess the circle part comes from its taste being this full, round flavor. And the red part . . . I don't even know how I know that.

"Evian is a blue triangle," I inform him.

"Yes! But what shade of blue?"

"Sky blue, duh."

"Can you believe some people don't know that?"

"Not really."

"What's Fiji?"

"Where Chuck Noland was stranded for four years."

"Who's Chuck Noland?"

"The character Tom Hanks played in *Cast Away*."

"Your memory is impressive," Jason says. "First my circles in algebra and now this."

"I like retaining information."

"So, hey. Your hiccups are gone."

I test it out. Ten seconds go by with no hiccups and no threat of impending hiccups.

"Finally," I go.

"And to think that you doubted my technique."

"I never doubted your technique."

"Are you sure about that? Because I thought—"

"Hey, Lani," Connor says, who's suddenly standing by our table. Except he's not in this lunch.

"Connor!" I go. "What are you doing here?"

"Emergency snack break. I'm sure Ms. Liddell won't mind."

"She doesn't know you left?"

"Yeah, but I asked to go to the bathroom. I think she'd understand if I pick up a quick snack cake, eh?"

"Definitely," I agree. "Oh, do you guys know each other?"

"Hey, man," Jason goes. "Didn't we have gym together last year?"

"I think so." Connor studies Jason. "You're Jason, right?"

"Yeah."

"I'm Connor."

"From Canada."

"You've heard about me."

"I think everyone knows you're from Canada, Connor," I say.

"Is it that obvious?"

"Well . . ."

"Jeez, try to blend in and you still get labeled. Anyone want a Coffee Crisp?"

"Huh?"

"Sorry, Canadian inside joke with myself. I'll be going now."

The next day in art, I'm searching the shelves for the clear glue when Connor comes over all determined. It's obvious he wants to say something. But he just stands there.

"Yeah?" I go.

Connor's like, "What? Nothing. I didn't say anything."

"But you're obviously going to."

"No, I was just looking for . . ."

"For what?"

"Graph paper."

"It's not with the other paper?"

"Oh. Right. I guess I should check over there."

"Are you okay?" I've never seen Connor all jittery like this.

"Couldn't be better. Well, it's possible I had too much sugar for breakfast."

"Really?" I go back to searching for the clear glue. "What'd you have?"

"Um. Pop-Tarts."

"I thought you hated those."

"And with good reason! I should have learned never to touch

those things again from my last sugar high." Then Connor goes off in search of some graph paper.

I finally find a bottle of clear glue shoved under a pile of felt. Back at my table, Sophie's working on some kind of pencil sculpture. She doesn't like talking while she's working, so I decide to ask her about it after class.

I inspect the carbon footprint awareness posters Danielle and I made last night. Today's a free day, so we can do whatever we want as long as it's art related. Ms. Sheptock and I have a deal that I can finish One World posters in here as long as I do something extra creative with them. I'm thinking sequins to outline the footprints we drew along the bottom of each poster.

Connor sits down across from me with his graph paper.

"What are you doing with that?" I ask.

"Don't know yet. I just had a feeling it was time for some intense graphics action. Maybe some anime."

"I didn't know you liked anime."

"I'm getting into it."

I trace the outline of one footprint with glue, then carefully press black sequins over it. I can feel Connor watching me.

"Stuck for ideas?" I go.

"You would make a great anime model," Connor says. "I mean, look at you."

I roll my eyes. "You're deluded." I had no idea Connor thought I was pretty. He's never said anything like that before.

"Mind if I sketch you?"

"Sure, as long as I can keep gluing these sequins."

Sophie takes a bottle of Poland Spring out of her bag.

"Red circle," I tell her.

"Huh?"

I point to her water bottle. "Poland Spring. It's like a red circle, right?"

Sophie stares at me like I'm speaking a whole other language. "Huh?" she goes again.

"No. I'm just . . . thinking of twenty things at once."

Sophie goes back to her pencil sculpture.

Everything always leads back to Jason. We connect in a way I've always hoped could be real. I've been wishing someone like him would come into my life for so long. Now's my chance to know what that kind of love feels like. How can I keep fighting it?

I could spend an eternity wondering if Jason's thinking the same thing. But there's only one way to know for sure.

17

It took me over a week to get the courage to do this. I couldn't concentrate on anything else for most of that time, thinking about what I should say, totally afraid of what might happen. Avoiding Erin was hard, but there's no way I could be hanging out with her while I was thinking about confronting Jason. I told her that I thought I was getting sick and I didn't feel like doing anything. Then I reminded myself that there's no way I could do this to her. I decided not to say anything to Jason.

But on Monday, my horoscope said that if I took a risk when I would normally play it safe, the payback would be immense. Magic 8 Ball agreed.

So I'm doing it. I'm going to ask Jason if he likes me. I have no idea what I'll do if he does. I just have to know.

Jason thinks I randomly ran into him instead of strategically placing myself down the hall from his last class. He's really high-energy today.

"You're in a good mood," I say.

"Totally."

"Just because, or—?"

"No, I started lifeguarding again Memorial Day weekend. I love getting back out there."

"Sweet."

"It really is. Hey, can we—"

"Jay-dog!" Greg comes over and pounds fists with Jason. "Where you been?"

"Nowhere."

"You going to Kaminsky's?"

"For that party?"

"It's gonna be killer. His parents are away all week."

Greg is totally ignoring me. I don't know if he knew that Erin was pushing me to like him before, but ever since I convinced her that it was never going to happen, it's like he doesn't even see me. Which is how some of the other Golden Kids treat me now, so I'm not all that surprised.

"Erin told me," Jason says. "We might be there."

"You *might* be there?" Greg is incredulous. "What's that about?"

Jason glances at me. Greg doesn't notice. Or he pretends he doesn't notice.

"I'll see you there," Jason goes. I can tell Jason's just trying to get rid of Greg.

"Later," Greg says. Of course he doesn't say bye to me or anything.

I say, "Can you believe he—" and Jason says, "Can we—" at the same time.

"You first," I tell him.

"Can I talk to you?"

"Yeah."

"Not here." Jason pulls on the door handle of the classroom next to us. The door's unlocked. We go in and close it behind us.

My nerves clang around, aware that we're all alone.

"Some light would be good," I say.

"Really? Because I was thinking light is so overrated."

It's a cloudy day and the windows have eastern exposure, so it's all dim in here. Actually, it's cool in a moonlit kind of way.

"You're right," I agree. "Not sure what I was thinking there."

Jason smiles my favorite Jason smile. It's the one where his eyes light up, like we have a secret. This is a perfect time to ask him. But maybe I should see what he wants first. He's never pulled me into an empty classroom before.

His smile slowly fades. His eyes change from aqua green-blue to deep sea green.

It's really hard to breathe when he looks at me this way.

"Um . . ." Jason goes. "So . . . I like you."

"Okay . . ."

"No, I mean . . . I *like* you like you."

Oh my god.

I go, "Why didn't you say anything before?"

"I thought you were going out with Blake, remember?"

"But why?"

"You know that time we went out for pizza?"

"Yeah . . ."

"I thought you guys were together."

"Why?"

"Just the way you were acting. He put his arm around you and stuff."

"But Blake is gay!" I shout.

Then I slap my hand over my face.

It's too late.

I just said the most secret thing I promised to never say.

"Please don't tell anyone that." I glance around, even though we're the only ones in here.

"I won't."

"No, you don't understand. No one. Can know. About Blake."

"Don't worry, I get it."

"His dad would *kill* him. Seriously."

"Lani. Don't worry. I won't tell anyone."

"Promise?"

"Promise."

"So . . . you didn't say anything because you thought Blake was my boyfriend?"

"Yeah. Erin just said you guys were her friends and I assumed you were together. I mean, I never asked her, but she never said you weren't. And I heard you were going out from some other people."

"Who?"

"People." He shrugs. "Around."

"But you asked me if we were going out and I said no."

"But by time—"

"—you were already with Erin."

"Exactly."

I cannot believe he just told me he likes me right before I was going to ask him the same thing. I should be used to these non-coincidences by now.

"Do you . . . feel the same way?"

This is it. I can deny my feelings and go on pretending that we can just be friends. I can try to keep everything the same. I can try to keep Erin from hating me for falling in love with her boyfriend.

But of course I can't do that. Everything is different now. My fate has been decided.

"Yeah," I say. "I like you, too."

"You do?" He has the biggest smile ever.

"You couldn't tell?"

"Not really. Well, I thought maybe you did, but I wasn't sure if it was all in my head. Like how much of it was really there instead of just what I wanted to see, you know?"

"Totally! I felt the exact same way!"

All along, I knew he liked me. But that knowing was deep down, squelched by insecurities. Your heart always knows, even if the truth is too hard to admit. The truth can never be denied.

Jason goes to push some hair off my face. My bangs get swept to the side.

I pull back from him. "Don't," I say.

"What's wrong?"

If he pushes my bangs back, he'll see my scar. I can't think of anything that would gross out a potential boyfriend more.

Wait. What am I thinking? *Potential boyfriend?* Am I crazy?

It's one thing to admit the truth about how you feel. It's a whole other thing to take it to the next level.

Jason looks confused, like he wants to know what he did wrong.

I go, "I have this . . . scar . . . on my forehead. From the accident."

"Can I see?"

"No! It's really gross."

"Oh. Can I see it anyway?"

"Why?"

"I just want to see your whole face."

I can't believe he wants to see my scar. And I can't believe I'm standing here, letting him push away my bangs to see it. But Jason doesn't look grossed out or anything. His expression doesn't even change.

I pull away from him again and shake my bangs back over my forehead. "I told you."

"Well, you're wrong. That scar has character. It has rock-star quality."

"I hate it."

"But you're so beautiful."

This is too much. Jason thinks I'm beautiful. Even with my face all ripped apart, he still thinks that.

I want to tell him everything I've been thinking and feeling, but I can't. Which really sucks. It sucks how Erin and I are both falling in love with him, but he's only falling in love with one of us.

Jason's standing so close to me. It's obvious that he's going to kiss me. And all I want to do is kiss him back.

part two

june–august

"A person often meets his destiny on the road he took to avoid it."
— Jean de La Fontaine

"You've got to take a chance on something sometime, Pam." —Jim Halpert

18

How could I do this to her?
She saved my life.

19

When Erin and I were ten, her mom was driving us back from Girl Scout camp. A huge storm had suddenly moved in that last day. It was a good thing that our tents and everything were packed up before the downpour hit.

Riding home was really scary. I could hardly see anything out the windows. The windshield wipers were almost invisible. They were madly smacking at the rain, struggling to push heavy sheets of water off the glass.

We were almost home when Erin's mom leaned forward really close to the windshield. She said, "I can't see the road."

I started to cry. Erin told me not to worry. She said we would be home soon.

"I'm going to try to pull over," her mom said. "We can wait for the storm to pass."

Putting on her blinker was useless. We had no idea if there were cars ahead of us or behind us. It was one huge water wall wherever you looked. Sometimes we'd see a blurry glow of light, but only for a few seconds.

Erin's mom wanted to get us over to the side of the road, but none of us could see where that was. All of a sudden, it felt like we were skidding. Later I learned that the car was hydroplaning.

Then there was a crash. It felt like we had smacked into something. I thought we had run into the car in front of us, except we were still moving. But not like driving moving. More like wobbling.

"Oh my god!" Erin yelled. "We're in the lake! Open your door!"

I tried to open my door. I pushed and pushed against it, but it wouldn't open. Neither would Erin's.

Erin's mom didn't say anything. She was hunched forward over the steering wheel. She wasn't moving.

"Mom?" Erin said, tapping her on the back. *"Mom?"*

The car rocked back and forth. The front end began to tip forward. A weird wooshing sound surrounded us.

"Try your window!" Erin yelled at me. She sounded really far away, even though she was sitting right next to me.

We pressed our window buttons. Nothing happened.

The front end of the car tipped forward some more.

The next thing I remember, the car was filling with water. The dashboard was almost submerged.

"We're drowning," I said. It was hard to get the words out. I was crying really hard.

Erin tried to pull her mom out of the front seat, but she couldn't. She could only pull her back enough so that her mom was leaning against the window. Water sloshed all over her mom's lap. The whole front of the car was filling with more water. Since the car was tilted forward, there wasn't as much water in the back.

"Mom!" Erin screamed. "Wake up!"

Erin's mom didn't move.

"Come on!" Erin told me. "Get in the back!"

I unclicked my seat belt and twisted around to climb into the back of the car. The car lurched forward. The metal part of the headrest slammed into my forehead.

I can't remember what happened next. All I know is that Erin and I were hunched together in the back of the car for eons. More and more water sloshed over us. The front of the car was almost totally submerged. Erin's mom was up to her neck in water. But there was more space in the back where we could breathe. Erin told me to keep my head above the water.

I focused on her.

I focused on breathing.

The car was found pretty soon after we went into the lake. It felt like a thousand years later, but my parents said the car was underwater for less than half an hour. Someone saw us go into the lake and called 911. So we got out okay. Erin's mom was okay, too, just unconscious until we got to the hospital.

I don't know how that person saw us. It had to be fate. Our lives were saved for a reason.

Big news travels fast in a small town. Everyone immediately heard about the accident. Tons of rumors were flying about us. There were so many versions of that day going around that I had to keep reliving what actually happened just to hold on to the truth. I had nightmares every night. I still have them sometimes.

When we got back to school, everyone was super nice. Girls who never talked to us before shared their candy and gave us stickers. One girl made us matching friendship bracelets that we wore for the rest of the year. Teachers gave us privileges. In social studies, I was allowed to pass out worksheets two days in a row and no one said anything. Even the boys stopped teasing us for a while.

These are the things that happen when you almost die but don't.

Though the details of the accident are probably hazy for most people by now, everyone remembers that Erin and I were in it together. They all assume that we'll be best friends forever. Because how can you share the most intense experience ever and not be soul sisters for life?

If Erin hadn't told me to, I don't think I would have climbed into the back of the car that day. I was so scared that we were going to drown. All I could do was sit there and cry. I was paralyzed by fear. But Erin made sure that I moved. She made sure that I kept my head above water. She kept me alive.

That's how much I owe her. I owe her my life.

20

When the camp bus pulls into the rec center's parking lot, all this gravel dust flies up into the air. It sticks to my sweaty skin. It gets in my eyes.

We're having a heat wave. It's supposed to be almost one hundred degrees today. For extra fun, it's crazy humid.

I really don't want to be here.

Erin wanted both of us to come with her to say good-bye. So Jason drove us over for Erin to catch her bus to sleepaway camp. Erin's stoked because this year she gets to be a leader-in-training.

She'll be in Vermont for two months.

Jason and I will be here.

Alone.

Parents are dropping kids off. Kids are dragging duffel bags across the gravel. Damp dust surrounds everything.

"I hope the bus is air-conditioned," I tell Erin.

"I know," she says. "It could not possibly be any hotter."

Jason reaches over and picks a piece of driveway off my arm.

I panic. I don't think he realizes what he just did. He's just standing there holding hands with Erin, squinting into the sun. Picking a piece of driveway off someone's arm is the kind of thing a close friend would do without even thinking about it. Except it's not that simple with us. Every time Jason's done something like that when Erin's around, I've panicked that she can tell.

I really wanted to kiss Jason the day he told me he liked me. I never wanted anything so much in my whole life. But of course I didn't kiss him. I'd never have been able to face Erin again. It's the worst kind of luck that she's already with the boy I want to be with. Or maybe fate got us confused.

Not kissing Jason that day was the hardest thing I've ever done. We just stood there in silence, looking at each other for a long time. Then he came closer, like he was going to kiss me. But I stepped back. I told him there's no way I could ever hurt Erin like that. You don't hook up with your best friend's boyfriend. Even if he breaks up with her first. Which I would never want to put her through, so it's pointless to even think about. I have to push those thoughts out of my mind and keep them there.

It's a freaking impossible situation with no solution.

Desperately scrambling to draw attention away from the fact that Jason just touched me, I stick out my arms and go, "I know, it's ridiculous! Look at all this dirt!"

Erin's squinting, too. But not from the harsh sunlight. She's squinting right at me.

Because she knows.

Wait. How can she know? It's not like there's anything *to* know.

I need to take the paranoia down a notch.

"Okay, you guys." Erin puts her bag down. She turns one of her rings a few times. "This is it. Next time you see me, we'll almost officially be seniors."

Jason's like, "Far out." He's still holding her hand.

Erin kisses him.

I look away, scuffing my flip-flop on the gravel.

"Don't forget to write," Jason says.

"You better write me!" Erin swats his arm. She's already made it clear that writing is mandatory. Cell phones and laptops aren't allowed at her camp. "I swear, if I don't get at least two letters a week, I'm coming back to kill you."

"Two letters a week!" Jason does this mock dying thing. "You're already killing me!"

"Oh yeah, right," Erin says. "Like that's a lot."

"Guys don't have that much to say," Jason informs her. "I'm sure Lani will write you all the time."

"Absolutely," I promise. It's the least I can do.

Kids start packing into the bus. A groan goes through the crowd. Someone found out there's no air-conditioning and it's a three-hour ride.

"Good luck with that," Jason tells Erin. He gives her a big hug.

Then I hug her. "I'll miss you."

"Me, too." Erin picks up her bag. Then she does a beauty-pageant wave. "Be good!"

We watch her find a seat on the bus. We watch the bus pull out. We stay until we can't see her anymore.

Erin seems so hopeful. Like when she comes back, everything will be exactly the same way she left it.

Like nothing will change while she's gone.

21

"*How does it* always know?" Blake marvels.

"Exactly!" I yell. "That's what I've been trying to tell you!"

Blake is *so* hooked on our weekly horoscopes. We've even established a new ritual for the summer. Blake comes over every Monday and we read each other our horoscopes. They can be a little tricky without school as a frame of reference, though.

Around here, you could totally avoid everyone all summer if you wanted to. It can be really desolate unless you make an effort to get together with people. The only people I'll probably see all summer are my parents, Blake, Danielle, and everyone at my summer job. I quit swimming class when school ended. I had a minor meltdown in my last class and made an executive decision to give up. So I've been pretty isolated. Which is a good thing.

We live in farm country. Not that we live on actual farms or anything. Well, a few kids from school have parents who are farmers, but they live in regular houses. It's just that New Jersey is called the Garden State because of all its farms. We have a lot of roadside markets selling fruit and vegetables. There are places open to the public that grow berries and pumpkins. I work part-time at Bear Creek Berry Patch over on Dark Moon Road. They grow all different types of raspberries. I didn't even know there was more than one kind of raspberry before I started working there last summer. My job is to help customers who come to pick their own berries. I also do some berry picking for the owners. It's cool because I can ride my bike there. Driving is something I only do when I have to. I hate contaminating the atmosphere with more pollution, plus wasting all that nonrenewable fuel makes me want to cry.

"This horoscope thing must be magic," Blake says.

"Or fate."

"As in, it's fate that they always know what to write?"

"Now you're getting it."

"Hmm." Blake scoots over to the other side of the couch. That area is closer to the ceiling fan, so it's like half a degree cooler over there. As usual, our central air is more like a random trickle of air that's not nearly cold enough.

I go, "How are we supposed to play now?"

"I can still reach."

Some people might think I'm a loser for hiding in my living room, playing 500 on a gorgeous summer day. That is just not true. It's actually a smart way to pass the time. This way, I'm not tempted to do other things. Other things that are potentially harmful.

Blake goes, "How's the berry business so far?"

"Oh, you know. Booming as usual."

"What's my favorite kind of raspberry that's—"

"Taylor."

"Yes! When are you bringing me some of those?"

"We don't pick them until August."

"That's just wrong."

"When are you bringing me your first professional creation?"

"Patience, my dear, patience." Blake got a summer internship at a glassblowers' studio. He got into glassblowing a few months ago. He saw these amazing glasses in a gift shop in town and asked where they came from. It turns out they were made a few towns over, by real glassblowers. Blake is psyched to be learning from them, but his dad is less than thrilled. He'd rather see Blake get a paying job and start earning his own money. They had a huge fight about it. I really thought Blake's dad was going to force him to work at Big Guy Burger. Somehow, Blake convinced his dad to let him take the internship. It makes me sad that his dad had to be convinced.

"Is your dad still in a huffufle about it?" I ask.

"Oh, he's huffufled, all right. Imagine if he knew I'm gay on top of making zero bank? The *horror*."

I wish there was a way for Blake to tell his dad who he really is. Things shouldn't be like this.

After Blake wins, I shuffle the deck to play again.

He's like, "So are you hiding in here all summer or what?"

"I go out. I go to work, don't I?"

"What about going out for fun?"

"I'm having fun with you."

"You're avoiding him."

"Who?"

Blake leans back on the couch. He watches the fan whir.

"You know who."

"No I don't."

"Let's see. He's about five nine, light-brown hair, green-blue eyes, is a lifeguard, is cute, rhymes with mason."

"You think I'm avoiding Jason?"

"Umm . . ."

"Because I'm not."

"Of course not. You're just . . . hanging out. Here. With me. Because it's so fun and all."

"You know I love hanging out with you."

"Has it ever occurred to you that you're in love with him?"

I stop shuffling. "It doesn't matter."

"Of course it matters. It's your life. You should stop fighting your feelings."

"What would be the point of that? He's my best friend's boyfriend, remember?"

"Yeah, but since when can we control who we love?"

He has a point. We can't help who we love. Blake knows that better than anyone. Love isn't logical, or even our choice.

Love chooses us.

After dinner, I help Mom wash the dishes. Dad's snoring on the couch. A crossword-puzzle book is splayed out over his chest.

"Mom?" I go.

"Is that dish towel too wet? There's another one—"

"No, it's fine. I wanted to ask you something about Dad."

She rinses a plate. "What is it?"

"Did you ever think . . . I mean, did you ever think that you were too different? You know, for things to work out?"

"Interesting question."

She's probably wondering where it came from. Of course, I could never tell her. What am I supposed to say? That I have way more in common with Jason than Erin does so I should be with him instead? Or since they don't have as much in common, why are they together?

"Well," Mom says, "some differences are important in a relationship. I don't think it's healthy for two people to spend all of their time together. That said, you definitely need to share some common interests. It's the things you have in common that connect you."

"But don't you guys have way more differences than similarities?"

"Maybe. But a few big similarities are more important than lots of little differences. You have to think about what's most important to you. If those things are most important to the person you're with, then you have the basis for a strong relationship. The small things don't matter as much." Mom looks over at Dad, snoring away on the couch. "I know it doesn't always seem like we're on the same page, but you have nothing to worry about. Your dad and I still love each other."

"Uh, that's—"

"Nothing's going to change."

It's like Mom thinks I'm asking because I'm scared they're going to get divorced or something. If I had the energy, I might explain that I'm not asking about them. But then she'd want to know why I'm asking, and then what would I say?

I don't know if Erin and Jason have enough important things connecting them. All I know is, Jason and I connect on so many different levels that it's like a whole new plane of existence. We have the kind of connection my parents can't even imagine. Or maybe they can, they just never found it.

If the psychic was right, I'll have more than one great love in my lifetime. Which means I'll get another chance. But is that any reason to throw my first chance away?

22

Here's the number-one reason why my summer job rules: I'm a berry freak. I have love for them in this order: raspberries, blackberries, blueberries, strawberries. I get these crazy cravings for them in the winter. Sometimes I even have these dreams where I'm right here at the berry patch, picking basket after basket like a fruit-starved maniac.

I've been helping a little girl pick raspberries for half an hour. She came with her older sister, but her older sister found something she liked more than berries. His name is Greg. Because of course Greg works here. He hates every minute of it, though. It's obvious that this is the only job he could find, the way he's constantly complaining about working outside in the broiling heat. I avoid the negative stressball that is Greg as much as possible.

"Try not to pick any soggy berries," I advise the girl. "Or ones with leaves."

When I get into the Berry Picking Zone, I kind of space out. I think about other things, working on automatic. I've been trying to avoid the Berry Picking Zone this summer. Especially today. Jason is all I try not to think about. Danielle invited me to this picnic at Green Pond, but I didn't go. I know Jason's a lifeguard there. I could probably find out what days he works and avoid going on those days. Or I could just not go there for the whole summer.

But What If? What if I'm doing the wrong thing? Is it really our fate to be apart?

After the sisters leave, I walk out deep into the field, away from everyone else. Right here, in the middle of everything, with the sweet summer breeze rustling through the leaves, I make a wish. I wish for the Energy to reveal my fate. To give me a sign if my fate is to be with Jason. And I promise myself that if I get a sign, I won't avoid the truth anymore.

23

Being lazy in the summer rules. It's awesome how everything slows down so you don't have to rush anywhere. It's like there's this unwritten agreement among everyone that it's okay to do nothing. The most strenuous activity I did today was making watermelon juice with Mom. Okay, she did most of the work. She got the watermelons at the green market and lugged them home and cut them up. But I was in charge of blending and straining. The taste of watermelon changes when you put it in the juicer, so we never do that. We also made watermelon, honeydew, and cantaloupe popsicles. Those are the best on scorching days like today.

It is such a major relief to not have any homework for the next two months. What would we do without summer vacay? Revolt, probably. It feels so decadent to have the entire summer ahead of me, a whole two months of staying up late and doing whatever I want. Like today, how I'm lazing in the hammock out in the backyard, reading the glossy magazines I love and drinking fresh watermelon juice. I should be totally blissed out.

There's just one problem.

I miss Jason.

It's been five days since I wished for my sign. Nothing's happened yet. Maybe nothing will. Maybe that's the way it's supposed to be. It just feels like something's missing. Like there's more to life that I haven't found yet.

"Transatlanticism" plays on my iPod for the third time.

I need you so much closer . . .
I need you so much closer . . .

The porch door slides closed, snapping me out of my daydreams. Mom wants me to get some things at the supermarket. Dad's not home, so I can't take his car. Which means I have to take the ancient stick shift.

I *hate* driving stick.

Dad's a patient guy. But when he was teaching me how to drive, there was this one time when he almost lost it. I was still learning how to shift without stalling in the middle of the street. Merging was completely hopeless. I'm terrified of merging. Merging is for people who can go out into the world and take charge. Merging is for people who laugh at fear. Merging is *not* for people who truly believe a truck will ram into them and flatten their car right when they get on the highway.

The day Dad almost lost it, I was creeping up on the road that feeds out onto the highway. He was like, "Get some speed going here."

I reluctantly pressed down on the gas pedal. I wished really hard that I was at home instead, but I was still in the car.

Then it was time to merge. My heart rattled.

"Get ready to merge," Dad went. Like it was nothing. Like he was saying, "Get ready for school." I wondered why he didn't know how traumatic merging was for me.

My arms and legs were shaking. My pulse raced.

I couldn't do it.

"What are you doing?" Dad yelled. "Merge!"

"I can't merge!" I yelled back. Cars honked behind us. We were next in line to merge. I just couldn't move into all of that speeding traffic.

"What the—? Pull over up here," Dad instructed. When we were pulled over, he went ballistic, saying how I could get myself killed if I'm too tentative. I've never seen him lose his temper that bad.

All the streets to the supermarket are tame, so my stress level remains tolerable. Even though it's an easy drive, I still manage to stall twice. At least no one's around to witness my lacking stick skills.

Mom's grocery list is all last-minute barbecue stuff. We have a party every summer for our neighbors. I usually hang out with this girl who lives up the street. We're not really friends. Everyone else who comes is either way older or way younger. It's not exactly a rager.

Most of the vegetables we're using for the salad and for grilling are from our garden. But there are a few things Mom doesn't grow, like cucumbers. So I'm inspecting the cucumbers for ones that are firm and medium green.

Someone comes over and picks up a cucumber. He taps it against the one I'm holding. This flash of annoyance cuts through me. I hate when guys bother me in random places. Especially creepy ones.

Then I realize that the cucumber tapper is Jason.

"Is this a good one?" he says. "I can never tell with these things."

"Cucumbers can be tricky."

"Is *that* what these are? I'm in the wrong place then."

"You got lost in the supermarket?"

"Must have taken a wrong turn around the Pop-Tarts. I was looking for raspberries."

"What?"

"Oh, you haven't heard of raspberries? They're awesome. How could you not know about them?"

"I know about them."

I must look totally freaked out. It's just so weird for him to say *raspberries* out of all the possible things he could have said. When I was just standing in the middle of all those raspberries a few days ago, wishing that my fate would reveal itself.

Obviously, it just did.

Jason's like, "Are you okay?"

I nod. There are no words.

"You sure?"

I nod some more.

"So . . . I have news," Jason goes.

"Is it good news or bad news?"

"Um, I'd say it's relative."

"How is it relative to me?"

"Hopefully, good news."

"Then I'm ready." I put the cucumber I was squeezing into my cart. I never knew being this nervous was possible.

"Okay, well . . . have you heard from Erin lately?"

"Yeah." I'm trying to remember when I got her letter. She's been gone for less than two weeks and I've only gotten one letter so far. I've sent her two already. "I got a letter from her three days ago."

"So she didn't tell you."

"Tell me what?"

Jason's eyes go dark green. "We broke up."

"Oh."

"So . . . yeah."

I want to ask things like who broke up with whom and why and when and how.

I ask none of these things.

Is he telling me this because he wants to go out with me? Doesn't he know that's impossible?

"Anyway," Jason says, "I just thought you should know."

I nod some more.

"We should hang out sometime."

"Yeah." I really want to. "Definitely." I really, *really* want to. But what would I tell Erin? In her letter she said I should hang out with Jason since she knows how you can get so isolated around here, but now everything's different. There's no way she would have written that now.

"Hey, so, can you explain about these cucumbers?" Jason says. "How do you know which ones are good?"

"Just don't pick any squishy ones and you'll be fine."

"Wow. I never knew it was that simple."

I check my list. "I have to get mayonnaise," I inform my shopping cart.

"I can watch your stuff if you want."

"Oh. Thanks." I leave my cart with Jason and go hunt down the mayonnaise. He must want to talk some more. Why else would he stay with my cart like that, when I could just wheel it over here myself?

The Energy is definitely bringing us together. Even when I was getting dressed this morning, it was strategizing. I live in these little sundresses all summer. I wear either a dress or shorts and a tank top pretty much every day. Today, I didn't reach for just any dress like I usually do. Something told me to put on my cutest one, which I hardly ever wear.

When I get back, Jason holds up a cucumber. "I found the best one." He looks extremely proud of himself.

I test the cucumber. "You're right. It is the best one. I better get it." I drop it in my cart. "Well . . . I should—"

"No, I have to go, too. It's not like I can stand around selecting produce all day."

I bite my lip.

"Jase, can you give me a hand?" his mom says, wheeling her cart over. I remember her from when we went to Jason's to make certificates after mentoring. "Oh, hi Lani. How are you?"

"Good," I say. I can't believe she remembers my name. I've only seen her that one time.

"One sec, Mom," Jason goes. Then he says to me, "So . . . I'll see you around?"

"Okay."

I lurch the car home in a daze. I unpack the groceries in a daze. I'm half unpacking, half staring out the window. Dad's in the backyard trying to figure out how the new environmentally friendlier barbecue works.

When I lift the cucumbers out of the bag, a piece of paper falls on the counter. I have no idea what it is.

After I unfold it, everything is clear.

Intelligence. Many issues sunshine sometimes. Yellow orange underneath.

There's no way to fight this anymore. I don't even want to.

I dial his number. He answers right away.

I say, "I miss you, too."

24

"*Are you sure* trains don't come this way?"

Jason keeps insisting that this part of the train tracks isn't used anymore. I keep asking if he's sure. Every few minutes it sounds like a train's coming, even though none ever do.

"Don't worry," he assures me again. "This branch hasn't been used since the seventies."

I stumble over some splintered wood.

Jason clutches my arm. "Do you really think I'd bring you anywhere that wasn't safe?"

"No."

"Trust me."

Electricity zings from where Jason's touching my arm, shooting in all directions. He must be feeling it, too.

Or not. He just goes, "There's a cool bridge up here."

We've already walked about two miles. I can see why Jason

loves walking the tracks so much. There are all these cool secret areas in the woods and old signs and hidden trails that you'd never see unless you were on this side of things.

"I used to play in that playground," Jason says.

"What playground?"

"See it? Through there?" Jason moves behind me. He points to where he's looking.

I only see endless green leaves. "Um . . ." I'm pressed up against him. I can smell the fabric softener in his shirt.

We swelter together in the heat.

I forget what the question was.

"Right there." He takes my hand and points with it.

Then I find snippets of the playground. Part of a sandbox. Some water spritzing from a fountain. A yellow Tonka truck.

"Oh!" I recognize it now. I'm just used to seeing the playground from the road, so it was hard to tell what I was looking at from way over here. "I used to play there, too!"

"Whoa." Jason backs away from me. He looks spooked.

"What?"

"Did you used to play in the sandbox?"

"I loved the sandbox."

"Did you have a red bucket and shovel with . . . some kind of pattern on them?"

"Smiley faces."

"Yes! Exactly!"

"How do you know that?"

"We played together. You let me borrow your bucket."

"Wait." I totally remember Jason now. He used to borrow my bucket to move like half the sand from one end of the sandbox to the other. Then he'd get water from the fountain and build these gigantic sand castles. Well, they seemed gigantic at the time. "Did I ask you why you didn't have your own bucket?"

"I think so."

"What did you say?"

"I don't remember."

"Me neither."

"But you remember me."

"Yeah. I really do."

This is too much. It's like we don't even have a choice about being together. Fate decided about us a long time ago.

Before I started learning more about concepts of fate, I would always be blown away when things like this happened. But the more I noticed them, the less surprised I was that these connections exist. Connections are all around us, and if we're open to them, we become more aware of them. So while I'm amazed, I'm not as shocked as Jason is. Of course we played together when we were little. It all makes sense now.

Some people think things like this only happen in movies. Like in *Broken English* when Parker Posey goes all the way to Paris looking for this guy and right when she gives up and she's taking the Metro to the airport, he gets onto her subway car. Doubters of fate see something like that and complain how those things never happen in real life.

But they do.

"So . . . why haven't we been friends this whole time?" Jason says.

"I don't know. I guess people grow up and go their separate ways."

"But we go to school together."

"Yeah, but how many classes have we had together?"

"But you were always . . . there."

I think Jason is starting to understand the power of fate. Or maybe he already knew, like I did, that the person he's meant to be with has been here this whole time.

We walk for two more miles, all the way to Green Pond Road. This is Jason's street.

"Do you feel like ice cream?" he says.

"When *don't* I feel like ice cream?"

"I'm guessing never?"

"Hey, you're good at this game."

There's an old-school ice-cream parlor near Green Pond called The Fountain. Since I'm doing stuff with Jason and, apparently, not trying to avoid him anymore, I can finally go there without worrying about running into him. Which is such a relief I can't even tell you. They have the best gelato ever. They also have this puffy purple couch I adore. It totally feels like you're sinking into a cloud when you lounge on it. I'm hoping that the couch is free. I've spent hours on that couch, wishing one day a boy I loved would be sitting there next to me.

Not that I love Jason or anything. I'm just psyched about the couch.

But I'm also worried that someone from school might see

us. Which wouldn't be a major issue if Erin and Jason were still together. No one knows they broke up yet, but if someone sees us and tells Erin when she gets back, she'll know we kept hanging out after Jason dumped her. How would I explain why?

When we go in, I'm relieved that no one we know is here. The couch is taken, though. I get a cup of honeydew gelato, and Jason gets a cup of watermelon gelato. I put my cup under Jason's nose and say, "Smell this."

He sniffs. "Whoa. That's intense."

"I know!" The honeydew gelato is so good. It smells like you just cut open a fresh honeydew. "I usually get watermelon, but I've been OD'ing on actual watermelon lately."

"Oh, totally. They're so good right now."

We sit at a window table. There's no way I'm eating outside. I am in desperate need of air-conditioning. We both are.

Before we take our first bites, we clink our spoons together and say, "Cheers." Then I go, "How's lifeguarding?"

"*So* good. It feels like . . . I don't know."

"What?"

"Like even if I'm just sitting there, I'm protecting everyone somehow. Just by watching them. And like, knowing I could save any one of them if I had to. It makes me feel like I'm doing something meaningful every day, you know?"

"Totally."

"It's kind of the same thing with the kids in mentoring. Like I'm helping them. When they talk to me about their problems and I can help solve them, it means I'm not just wasting my time. I'm doing something that matters to people."

I nod. It's the first time Jason has said anything like this. He's told me about some personal stuff, but he never really talks about his feelings. Mostly he keeps everything on a lighter level.

Then Jason goes, "How's swimming?"

"I'm not going anymore."

"You're done? Sweet!"

"No . . . more like, I quit."

"Oh. Why?"

Here's why: I almost drowned in my last class and totally overreacted. While I thought I was really drowning, I was actually in a part of the pool where I could have just stood up and I would have been fine. But ever since the accident, I completely spaz when water gets even remotely scary. It was just way too embarrassing, sputtering out of the water with everyone staring at me, all concerned. So I stopped going. The thing is, I still want to learn how to swim before my family reunion in Hawaii. I have a year left. Maybe I can find a different class where no one saw my meltdown.

There's no way I can admit all that to Jason. "I'm just not talented in that area," I tell him.

"False. Anyone can learn how to swim."

"How do you know?"

"Uh, I'm a lifeguard, remember? Drawing perfect circles isn't my only talent."

"Then why's it taking me so long to learn?"

"People learn at different rates, is all. I can totally teach you."

"Really?"

"Anytime. Just say the word."

"Maybe I will." How cool would that be? I bet Jason's a really good teacher. I saw how he was with the kids he mentors. He's patient and funny, which are the two most essential qualities for making learning easier. Plus knowing what you're doing, which he does. The downside would be that he'd see how pathetic I am and then he might not like me anymore. Swimming is obviously important to him. But maybe wanting to learn is enough, even if I suck at it.

I just want to be with him. I haven't heard from Erin about the breakup yet and there's no way I can even begin to tell her what's going on. She'd never understand.

I wish this didn't have to be so hard. Because I love how I feel when I'm with Jason. The way we are together. The way I can tell what he's thinking, just by the color of his eyes. Our secret sandbox history. It's like we were made for each other.

If this isn't something like fate, I don't know what is.

25

We decided to get here early to find the best spot. It's getting crowded now, so I spread out the blanket to its maximum capacity. Then I put our flip-flops along the bottom edge of the blanket.

"Staking out the territory," Jason says.

"I hate when people try to move into your space."

"I hear you. But don't worry. No one stands a chance against those flip-flops."

"Flip-flops are ferocious."

"Exactly." Jason smiles with his eyes all sparkling. Like they're lit up just for me. Then we're sitting there, looking at each other. Not saying anything. His smile starts to fade. "Hey, um . . ."

"Do you want a Popsicle? They have—oh, or a snow cone? *Love* those!"

"Sure. But I'm treating."

"That's okay." I jump up and slide on my flip-flops. "I've got it."

"You sure?"

"Totally. What kind do you want?"

"That's an excellent question. Hmm. Well, it *is* the Fourth of July. Do they have those red-white-and-blue Popsicles?"

"Oh, yeah! The ones that look like rockets?"

"Those are the ones."

"They better. I'll be right back."

I go over to the ice-cream truck with my heart skittering all around. I have this feeling like Jason was about to say something that I wasn't ready to hear. What am I going to say if he asks me out? I can't go out with him. He just broke up with my best friend.

Key words being *broke up.* Does that mean this is something like a date? Or that it *is* a date? Does Jason think I'm here with him because I want to be his girlfriend? As if I could even go there. I mean, hanging out as friends is one thing. But there's a line. And once you cross it, there's no going back.

When I come back with our Popsicles, the sun is setting behind the trees. We lean back on the blanket, watching. The sunset is pink and red.

"Cool," Jason says.

"I know."

"It's wild how the trees look like they're on fire." He points. "Like where they're reflecting the sunlight?"

Jason's the only boy who would ever understand about sunset-fire trees. Most boys don't even notice things like colors and light the way I do.

"So, you decided to go with the Fourth of July theme, too," he says.

"What?"

Jason points his Popsicle at my Popsicle.

I'm like, "Oh. Well, you inspired me, so I didn't have a choice."

"Cheers." He holds his Popsicle out to mine.

"Cheers." We tap them together.

We watch the sunset.

When the fireworks start, everybody cheers. There are all these blue-and-purple ones, plus red ones that are the exact shade of sunset red. There are ones that look like flowers exploding. Ones that look like green rain. My favorite ones are the hearts. And the smiley faces.

The best way to watch fireworks is lying back on a pillow. I only brought one pillow, so we're sharing. I put my favorite pillowcase on—the one with a black-and-white-striped cat wearing big red sneakers.

After the finale, everyone cheers again. Then it's this mad rush of people grabbing their stuff and packing up and shaking grass off their blankets. The guy next to us on Jason's side snaps his blanket in the air, flinging grass all over him.

Jason wipes grass off his nose. "Guess he didn't notice me sitting here."

"You're hard to miss."

"Thanks."

"Oh, please. As if anyone wouldn't notice you."

He has that look again. The one with the dark green eyes. The one where I can't breathe right.

"Let's stay," I tell him.

"Okay."

I don't want to leave. Ever. It's so perfect here, with the amazing night and the sky all big and the sweet summer breeze. It feels like the park is here just for us. Especially after everyone leaves. We're the last two people left, in the middle of everything. Just lying on the blanket and sharing my pillow, looking up at the big sky all around us. We're the only two people in the world.

I want something to happen, but at the same time I don't. I don't know what I want. Or I do. But I shouldn't want it.

"Firefly!" Jason goes.

"Where?"

"See it?" He points. "Over by—"

"Oh, yeah! There's another one!"

"They're coming back out now. The fireworks scared them away."

"I love fireflies!"

"I know."

Then we have a contest to see how many fireflies we can count. Which of course is a bogus contest, since they keep flying around in the same circles. There's no way to know which ones are which.

"Seventeen!" I yell.

"Disqualified. You counted that one already."

"How do you know which one I'm counting?"

"Come on. You obviously mean that one."

"Which one?"

"Oh yeah, right. Like you don't know which one."

Jason shifts a little. Now his head is touching mine. The part of my head touching his head is all tingly. Is he going to move his head away? Did he shift on purpose so we'd be touching like this? I want to keep my head touching his head, but I'm afraid I'm going to spaz and have one of those jerky twitches where you're ultra aware that part of you is touching part of someone else and you're trying too hard not to move.

Maybe I should just try to relax.

Crickets chirp. Stars slide into new positions. More fireflies blink on.

When Erin and I were little, we had firefly collections. This was before I realized that you shouldn't take living things out of their natural habitat and shove them into captivity. We'd go into my backyard and stretch out our arms and let the fireflies land on us. Or we'd chase after them, careful not to damage their wings. Actually, most of the females can't fly, but they all light up.

That lighting up is a signal to the other fireflies. They light up to say, "Hey. I like you. Let's be friends." Actually, I think they want to be more than friends when they do that. It got me thinking about the way we put signals out into the world for other people to see. To let them know we're lonely or that we're looking for new friends.

Or that we want a boyfriend.

Not that I'm necessarily looking. I mean, every girl I know wants a boyfriend or a girlfriend. Most girls I know want a boyfriend so badly it's all they can think about. They have this attitude like once they find him, their life will instantly be perfect. Like it never occurred to them that maybe the reason they feel lonely or sad or bored has to do with them, not with the lack of someone else.

"Lani."

"Hi."

"Hi. I'm having a really good time."

"Same here."

Jason moves his arm so it's touching mine. Okay. Now I *know* he did that on purpose.

He goes, "No, I mean . . . just being here with you."

"I know. I like it, too."

Then Jason moves his fingers over my hand. He bends his fingers around mine.

And then we're holding hands.

And I swear, the Earth stops rotating.

Should I say something? Or should I wait for him to say something? What if I wait and he doesn't say anything and he thinks I'm not saying anything because it's okay with me that he's holding my hand?

Is it okay that he's holding my hand?

Of course it's not okay. Erin would freak if she knew. Imagine you're Erin and you're away at camp, thinking you'll have this perfect boyfriend waiting for you when you get back. Then he tells you it's over. Before it really even started. How would you feel if he was going out with your best friend on top of all that?

You'd feel like dying. That's how you'd feel.

So how can I do this to her? How can I lie here like it's okay, with our heads pressed together on my pillow, holding hands?

I slide away a little so I can look at Jason. His eyes are closed.

I stare at his profile in the dark, memorizing it. The slope of his nose. The shape of his lips.

I don't know what's happening to me. I guess you get to a point where you can't fight it anymore. You just can't help it. Because it's taken control of you. And it's never letting go.

He opens his eyes. He turns toward me.

Our faces are really close. We stare at each other. He touches my cheek, brushing some hair away from my face.

"We can't do this," I say.

"Why not?"

"Erin's my best friend."

"So, she wants you to be happy, right?"

"Yeah, but—"

"Lani," he whispers. "We belong together."

And then he kisses me.

There's no time to think about it.

There's no way to take it back.

Our lips stay pressed together, like neither of us wants to be the first to move away.

We stay on our blanket, holding hands. I don't know how much time passes. It's the most intense night of my life. I don't want to worry about it. I just want to experience how this feels right now, the way it never will again.

But then I suddenly remember that I told my mom I'd be home by eleven.

"What time is it?" I whisper.

Jason lets go of my hand. He presses a button on his watch. The screen lights up.

He's like, "Whoa."

"What?"

"That can't be right."

"*What?*"

"What time did you say you had to be home?"

My stomach sinks. "Eleven. Why?"

"It's one fifteen."

"Shut up."

He shows me his watch.

I'm dead meat.

"Just call your mom." Jason takes out his cell. "Ask if you can stay longer."

"There's no way she'd let me stay."

"It's safe. There's no one here."

"Exactly. So if some crazy slasher dude sneaks up behind us, we're toast."

"That's not happening."

"How do you know?"

"It's just not. And if it did, which it's not, I'd protect you."

"From crazy slasher dude?"

"From anyone."

I *so* don't want to leave. I want to stay here forever, just like this. But if I don't call my mom and get home, she'll kill me. If crazy slasher dude doesn't kill me first.

"I have to go," I tell him. "Can you drive me?"

"Of course."

Jason looks exactly how I feel. Well, maybe not exactly. We're both crushed that we have to leave. But I might be the only one who feels guilty.

26

"*What's a nine-letter* word for 'trinket or bibelot'?" Dad asks. He loves cracking into a new crossword-puzzle book. Whenever he starts his first crossword puzzle in a new book, we always work on it together.

"Knickknack?" I go.

"That's ten letters."

"Hmm." I yank on a particularly stubborn corn husk. It just does not want to part with its corn. Husking corn is always messier than you think it's going to be, so I'm husking on the back-porch stairs with a bucket between my legs. Dad's on the swing, determined to get this puzzle done before dinner. "It can't be doodad."

"Tchotchke!" Dad blurts.

"Nice one."

"Thank you, thank you."

I like these times with my dad. We don't really talk that much, so the other ways we connect mean a lot to me. I guess we talked more when I was little. That was mostly me babbling and him listening, though. Dad used to take me to work with him sometimes. I loved watching him build greenhouses. The best part was right after a greenhouse was finished, before the plants went in. I remember standing in the middle of all that glass and light, feeling like I had my own magical kingdom. Then the plants would come in all around me and I totally felt connected to them. Those early experiences inspired my love for all that is green.

I take a deep, sniffing breath. "This corn smells so good!"

"Umm," Dad goes, trying to figure out the next clue.

"I can't wait for dinner!"

"You're in a good mood."

"I'm usually in a good mood."

"True enough. But there's something extra good about it today."

Can he tell where my good mood is coming from? I hope not. It's not something I could ever talk about with Dad. He's left all of the boy-related discussions, including The Talk when I was eleven, up to Mom.

Jason and I have been seeing each other every day we can. He makes me feel alive in a way I always hoped was possible. Of course, we can only be together the way we want when no one else is around. We've seen a few kids from school, but they either already knew we were hanging out or didn't care.

Oh, wait. Greg cares.

We were at work today when Greg came at me all like, "Did I see you with Jason at The Fountain last night?"

Greg knows that I know he saw me. If he has a point, he's going to have to be more explicit.

"I don't know," I say. "Did you?"

"Unless that was someone else hiding out at a corner table with him, then I think I did, yeah."

I go back to picking raspberries. I get to take two pints home today, so I want to concentrate on finding the biggest ones.

Greg's like, "Uh, we're having a conversation here?"

"Are we? I thought you were just telling me where I was last night. Thanks for the reminder, by the way."

"You need to drop it."

"Drop what?"

"Whatever it is you're trying to do. He's already with Erin."

Okay. This is weird. Jason and Greg are friends. So why wouldn't Jason tell Greg that he and Erin broke up?

I'm not going to be the one to break the news.

I go, "In case you haven't noticed, Erin's my best friend."

"Yeah," Greg went. "Right."

I avoided him for the rest of the day.

How weird is it that you can be so happy and so frustrated at the same time? I just want to be with Jason for real. But no one can know what we really are.

My parents definitely can't. They totally freaked when I stayed out late at the fireworks two weeks ago. They were doing the whole Waiting Up thing when I got home. It was actually the first time they ever had to wait up for me because I'd never missed curfew before. I thought they'd go easier on me since it was my first major offense. I was wrong. They said they were disappointed in me. They demanded to know who I'd been out with. I had told them that I was going to see the fireworks with Blake and Danielle and some other kids from One World, but when I wasn't home by midnight my mom called Blake's dad. I was grounded for a week. Plus, now I have a set 11:00 curfew, whereas before it was more flexible.

My parents know I hang out with Jason. It's just that they think we're only friends. At least, I think that's what they think. They haven't said anything about it. After I told Blake about the Fourth of July fiasco, he said he'd cover for me from now on. Blake's the only one I can trust with the truth.

Hiding the truth has to end sometime, though. Every time I get a letter from Erin, my heart sinks. I'm dreading the day she finds out what's really going on.

When I got her first letter, I put it on my desk and spent the rest of the day avoiding it. I chopped up watermelons and made juice. I went to work and picked nine pints of raspberries. I came home and took a nap in the hammock. I woke up all sweaty and cooled off in the outdoor shower my dad built last summer. We ate dinner out on the back porch. I got corn stuck in my teeth and had to floss after. When I got back up to my room, the letter was still waiting there for me to open it, all impatient.

"Yeah, yeah," I muttered. "Keep your flap on."

I knew I had to open the letter. I had to open it and read it and deal with what it said, even though it was going to be bad. What else would I expect Erin's first letter after Jason broke up with her to be like? Sparkly rainbows and smiley faces?

No. More like dark clouds and torrential downpour. And I really didn't want to be stuck in the storm.

But I already was. So I took the letter over to my bed and sat down and forced myself to read it. I could not have felt worse for Erin. My heart hurt for her. She sounded miserable, describing how Jason wrote her this two-page letter about how it's him, not her. He told her that she's great and all, but he didn't think they were the right people for each other. He thought she would be happier with someone else. Which obviously meant that *he* would be happier with someone else.

"Like that's ever going to happen!" Erin wrote. "How am I supposed to trust anyone ever again?"

She had a point. As far as Erin knew, everything was going great with Jason up until he dumped her. Plus, she had no idea I was involved. Which is the worst part of all.

A few days later, I got another letter. That one was different. Erin told me about this boy Lee and how they hung out at a dance her camp had with the boys' camp from across the lake. And how these two camps have activities together every week and she can't wait for the next one, which is movie night.

The letter never mentioned Jason.

Erin's letters just got happier from there. They've been filled with more exciting news about camp and Lee and how much fun she's having. She just sounds like a totally different person. If she's still upset about Jason breaking up with her, she's really good at hiding it. It seems like she's swept up in the whole summer camp–romance thing with Lee and the intensity of it has obliterated the pain of Jason dumping her.

Now that she has Lee, I think we can finally tell her about us. Jason doesn't agree.

"I don't think that's a good idea," he says.

"We can't put it off forever," I say. "If she finds out we hid this from her, it's just going to make her angrier."

"I get what you're saying, but I already broke up with her in a letter. I don't think another letter with more bad news is the way to go. We should wait until she gets back so we can tell her in person."

Jason rows some more. We're taking the rowboat out on the lake. I'm terrified. I never agreed to let Jason teach me how to swim, but he's doing our first lesson anyway. When I heard it didn't involve actually getting wet, I said okay. The point of this lesson is for me to start trusting the water. Jason says that's the first step in learning how to swim. He says that if you can't trust the water, you'll never let go.

The boat rocks back and forth a little. I grip the sides like we're going under.

"Don't worry," Jason says.

"I'm not," I go, still gripping.

"Didn't I tell you I'd protect you?"

"Yes."

"Well, there you go. You're totally safe."

"Are you sure?"

"Come on. Would I promise to protect you if I couldn't guarantee your safety one hundred percent?"

"No?"

"Correct."

We go out really far on the lake. Or at least it feels far.

"Okay, now . . ." Jason stops rowing. We probably look like tiny dots from my house, floating on the calm water in the middle of everything.

"Take a deep breath," Jason goes.

I take a shallow breath. I'm too nervous to inhale more air than that.

"Just breathe," he says quietly.

I try to. After a few minutes, my stress level goes from a ten-plus to about an eight.

I manage to look around without moving too much. It's really pretty out here. And it's cooler, which is a definite bonus. It's like we're in our own private world. Like when I'd stand in the middle of those new greenhouses when I was little, looking up into the sky.

Jason's like, "Sshhh!"

"I didn't say anything," I whisper.

"What's that sound?" he whispers back, all serious.

"What—"

"Wait!"

We listen. All I hear is a mourning dove. They have a really specific hooing sound that always relaxes me. My stress level goes down to a seven.

"You mean the mourning dove?" I go.

"No, it's . . ." Jason leans over the water. I grip the sides of the boat again. "It's the water. Hear it?"

"Not really."

"It's saying, 'Lani, be one with me,'" Jason goes in a burbly voice.

"Shut up!" I let go of the boat for two seconds to swat him. "You speak Water?"

"Of course. It's an integral part of lifeguard training."

I roll my eyes. He's such a dork.

Jason still thinks the joke is funny. "The water wants to connect with you."

"As long as I can do that from up here in the boat, I'm good."

"You can put your hand in."

I release my grip on the boat and stretch my fingers down toward the water. I dip my hand in.

"Ooh," I say.

"Feels nice, right?"

"Yeah." I picture what it would be like to swim in the lake, surrounded by all that smooth, cool water. I can almost imagine it. What I can't imagine is how I'll ever have the courage to get past my fear.

27

This is the hottest day ever. It's about a hundred and twenty in the shade. If I had to work today, I'd probably pass out from heatstroke. All I want to do is sit on the couch with the fan in front of my face and read my new book.

But that's not happening. What's happening is that I have to go help Mom in the garden. She's making me. I tried to argue that reading is an important skill, so I should get to stay inside. Mom argued back that facing the world is also an important skill, so I should help her in the garden unless I want my 11:00 curfew moved to dinnertime. She's been crazy strict ever since the Fourth of July incident. I swear, she's never letting that go.

I put on a huge straw hat. I slide the porch door open. A wall of hot humidity immediately slams into me. I can hardly breathe.

The sun is relentless. It's funny how I used to make fun of Mom's schlumpy gardening hats. Now I totally wear them.

Mom's straw hat is even bigger than mine. It has ridiculous felt vegetables all around the rim. I am completely mortified. Good thing the garden is out back where no one can see us.

We work in silence. It's too hot to talk. But even with the oppressive heat, I feel like I have to talk about Jason or I'll explode.

"Can I ask you something?" I go. "Hypothetically?"

"Great idea. It'll help take our minds off this heat."

"I told you it was too hot!"

"Oh, it's broiling. But the garden can't be ignored."

"So back to my question. Say you're . . . at the green market. And someone—"

"You're coming with me this weekend, right?"

"I'm there." Sometimes I help Mom at the green market, where she sells her vegetables (including tomatoes, even though they're technically fruit). The whole town goes crazy over Mom's tomatoes. She could seriously rule one of those hokey vegetable competitions if we had any around here. I can picture her holding up a giant trophy with a gold-plated tomato on top, which is only a slightly less mortifying image than Mom in her vegetable gardening hat.

"Anyway," I go, "say you're at the green market and someone comes up to you and they want the best tomatoes you have. So you sell them, like, five of your best ones." I pull at a stubborn weed that's not budging. It must be a fellow Taurus. "But then later, someone else comes over and says that they heard how you sold your best tomatoes to so-and-so, but they deserve the tomatoes more because they *really* love tomatoes. And that other person hardly ever eats tomatoes. She'll probably let the tomatoes go bad."

Mom puts down her trowel. "But I already sold the tomatoes."

"True, but this other person thinks they deserve them more."

"Well, too bad, they're already gone."

This isn't coming out right. I can't talk about Jason by actually talking about Jason, so I thought up this tomato analogy. Somehow, it made more sense in my head.

Mom looks at me. "You think I should get the tomatoes back? That person's probably home by now."

"No." I finally pull the stubborn weed out with a final decisive yank. "It's stupid. Forget it." I'm not even sure what I'm trying to ask anymore.

The backs of my knees are all sweaty. I stand up to stretch my legs.

"They both have a right to those tomatoes," Mom says, "even if one of them likes tomatoes more."

"Forget the tomatoes. Okay, like . . . say a friend of yours has a pet. A dog. And every time you go over, the dog gets all happy because he obviously likes you more. Maybe the dog is allergic to your friend and really shouldn't be living there in the first place. So your friend gives you the dog because she knows he'll be much happier with you."

"What kind of dog is it?"

"He's a . . . French bulldog. So you assume everything is going to be fine from now on, but then your friend gets mad at you because you have her dog."

"That she gave me."

"Yeah. But now she's mad at you for taking him and she wants him back. What would you do?"

"I guess it would depend on how attached to the dog I was."

"Extremely attached. You love this dog."

"How much does my friend love the dog?"

"Why does that matter? He's miserable with her."

"But this isn't about the dog, is it? It's about the friend."

As usual, my mother is annoyingly right. I know Erin's going to be mad at me. I just have to hope that it won't last too long.

Five lifetimes later, we're done with the garden. I go straight for the outdoor shower. My dad is genius for building this, especially because it runs on solar power. It's so hot out that the cold water only gets cool, so I don't even touch the hot-water faucet.

The rest of the day is a fog of groggy indoor activities. There's no way I'm going back out until much later tonight. When I'm not supposed to.

Having an 11:00 curfew is bogus. How can anyone think that's late when it's not even a school night? Eleven is nothing. There's no way I can be expected to stick to that. It's so unfair. Everyone I know has a 1:00 curfew this summer. Even Danielle's parents let her stay out until midnight, and they're way strict.

So I don't feel that bad about sneaking out to be with Jason.

Staying in my room would be pointless. There's no way I'd be able to sleep. All I'd do is lie in bed awake half the night, aching for him. Since I'm going to be awake anyway, I might as well enjoy it.

The third stair from the bottom is creaky. If I go downstairs slowly and stay close to the wall and avoid the creaky stair, I should be able to get out without waking up my mom. My dad could sleep through the apocalypse.

Holding my flip-flops, I sneak down the stairs. I'm sure the neighbors can hear my heart pounding. When I get to the fourth stair from the bottom, I slide my left leg down so I can skip the creaky stair, desperately clinging to the wall. I'm too short for these kinds of contortions.

When I finally make it to the bottom of the stairs, I nervously look up to the second floor, expecting Mom to bust out of her room and ground me for life. But nothing happens. I don't hear anything.

I sneak out the back door.

So this is what the world is like when everyone else is sleeping. The oppressive humidity of the day is mostly gone. It's at least ten degrees cooler. All I hear are crickets. Fireflies are all around. I could get used to exploring the world at night.

Jason's waiting for me at the end of my driveway. He looks as happy as I feel. I run the rest of the way, which is not easy to do in flip-flops. I slam into him and hold on tight.

"Whoa," Jason goes. "Hi there."

"Hi."

"Ready?"

"Always."

Jason parked his Jeep far enough down the road so no one

would hear him start it. We get in. He got this old Jeep when he turned seventeen. It's kind of beat-up, but he's proud of it. I like riding in it with the wind whipping all around. Sometimes it gets scary when we're going down a jagged dirt road. It feels like the whole thing is about to shatter into a thousand pieces. But you know. It's scary in a thrilling sort of way.

The Jeep's roof is off. The warm wind whips all around us. We have the whole town to ourselves.

If life could always be as perfect as this, there would be no hate.

Jason's cell rings.

"I thought I turned that off," he goes. He takes it out of the cup holder and checks the screen. "Crap. It's Greg."

"We're not here."

"No, he left a message before about some party and I didn't call him back. He'll harass me all night if I don't talk to him."

From what he's told me, Jason hasn't been talking to Greg that much. That's why he didn't tell Greg about breaking up with Erin. Jason hasn't even seen him since the breakup.

Jason pulls over. He says, "Hey," into the phone.

Greg is yelling so loudly that I can totally hear him. "Dude!" he yells. "Where you at?"

"I'm not coming," Jason tells him.

"What?" Greg yells. Music is blasting in the background. "I can't hear you!"

"I said I'm not coming!"

"Why not?"

"I'm busy."

"With what?"

"With stuff. I'll make it to the next one."

"Get your ass over here!" Greg yells.

"I gotta go."

"What?"

"I'll talk to you tomorrow!"

"You suck!" Greg yells.

Jason snaps his phone closed.

"Did you want to go to that party?" I ask. "Because I don't mind."

"Well, *I* mind. Does any of that sound remotely fun to you?"

"Um, no?"

"Good answer," Jason says. "There's a reason you're pretty much the only one I've been hanging out with this summer."

At first I thought it was kind of strange that Jason doesn't have a best friend, but now I get it. Jason's friends with a lot of people. It's just that he doesn't really connect with any of them on a deeper level. We're the only ones who get each other the way we've always wanted to be gotten.

When we come over the top of the hill, the huge moon is looming in front of us. I've never seen the moon this big. It's so big it's almost scary.

"It's like an early harvest moon," I marvel.

"I've heard of those, but I have no idea what they are."

"It's the full moon closest to the autumnal equinox." I don't say what the harvest moon means astrologically. It represents a time of clearing up emotional issues. It's a time for forgiving yourself and letting go of baggage to prepare for new growth. None of which I'm ready to do. Good thing it's not a real harvest moon.

The moon's all massive and orange on the edge of the horizon.

"It just rose a few minutes ago," Jason says. "That's why it looks so big. It's an optical illusion."

"I know." When the moon is close to the horizon, your mind compares it with other objects you're seeing around it, like trees and houses. If the moon always looked this big, it would be awesome. There would be some serious moonlight all the time.

"I wish it could always be like this."

"I was just thinking that."

I lean against Jason, watching the moon, trying to hold on to how all of this feels. I don't ever want to forget any of it.

28

It's impossible to believe that school starts in two weeks. I have absolutely no idea where the summer went. I guess that's what happens when you're in love. Time plays tricks on you.

I agreed with Jason that we'd tell Erin about us when she got home. She's staying longer at camp for a training session so she can be a counselor next summer. Ever since Greg confronted me about seeing us together, we haven't done much in public. Jason would rather avoid everyone than risk Erin finding out before we tell her. We've only gone to the movies once and we've been avoiding The Fountain. The few times we've seen kids from school, we've acted casual. Today Jason's lifeguarding at Green Pond. I'm laying out (close to Jason's post, but not too close), which is totally harmless since I probably won't even talk to him.

But the second we're alone, we can't take our hands off each other.

The only thing I can think about is kissing Jason. My skin burns to touch him. It's like a fever. I'm so distracted even when I'm doing simple things, like helping Mom in the garden. One time I yanked out a tomato plant when I was weeding.

I am insane.

Nights are when we can be together for real. These summer nights with Jason are the most intense ever. It's impossible to imagine experiencing anything remotely close to them again. I already know that I'll remember this time of my life forever, no matter what happens. I've snuck out a few more times to see him. So far, we haven't been caught.

I can't wait for tonight. When we can finally be alone. When I can kiss him for hours.

The waiting is torture.

I need to put more sunblock on. My skin is totally crispy. I'm sure it would probably feel great to get in the water, but that's not happening.

Almost everyone is in the water. It's scorching hot today. I spray more sunblock on, especially around my bikini top. I usually don't spray carefully enough there and then I get sunburned along the edges of my straps.

Jason's up in his tall lifeguard chair, watching the water. He looks really good today. I mean, he looks good every day, but there's something extra cute about him today. All I want to do is climb up the ladder and sit with him. It would be so awesome if we could just be boyfriend and girlfriend like everyone else. How can two people have a legitimate relationship if no one else knows about it?

Jason catches me looking at him. He smiles. We both have sunglasses on, but I can see his exact eye color, burned into my memory.

"Hey, Lani," Connor says. "Is this spot taken?"

"It's all yours." I've seen Connor out here a few times before. He always comes over to say hi, but this is the first time he's sat next to me. I wish Blake could be here, but he has glassblowing almost every day, while I only work a few days a week.

Connor spreads his towel out. It has a moose and two guys on it.

"What's that moose?" I ask.

"Oh!" Connor laughs. "I've had this forever."

"Who are those guys with him?"

"Bob and Doug." From the way he says this, it's like I should know who Bob and Doug are.

"Who are they?"

"You don't know Bob and Doug McKenzie?"

"Not so much."

"Jeez!" Connor tells me all about them. Apparently, they're big in Canada. Something about donuts and hosers and tuques.

I'm like, "What's a tuque?"

"Oh, yeah. I keep forgetting they don't call them that here. It's a winter hat."

"Then why don't you just call it a hat?"

"It's a special hat. It has a pom-pom."

"Well, if it has a *pom*-pom . . ."

Connor puts on industrial strength sunblock. "How's the water?" he says.

"I hear it's great."

"You haven't gone in yet?"

"I'm not going in."

"Why not? It's like a thousand degrees out!"

"I like the heat." That's such a lie. But I'd rather lie than have to explain where my fear of water comes from. Connor probably doesn't know about the accident. By the time he moved here, it was ancient history in the gossip department.

I spend the next few hours flipping through my glossy magazines and sweating more than I thought was humanly possible and talking to Connor and sneaking looks at Jason. When it gets unbearably hot, I start packing up my stuff.

Connor goes, "Can I ask you something?"

"Sure."

"Do you . . . um, would you . . . do you want to do something sometime?"

Oh, no. I had a feeling this was coming. Ever since that day in art last year when Connor sort of said I was pretty, I've been scared he was about to go there.

Still, I should clarify. "You mean . . . like . . . a date?"

"Yeah."

See, here's where it gets complicated. It's not like I can come right out and tell Connor that I have a boyfriend. He'll want to know who and then what would I say? So how do I tell him that I'm unavailable without explaining why?

The only person who knows the truth about Jason and me is Blake. I know I can trust him not to tell Erin or anyone else. At first, I wasn't going to tell anyone about us. But I was dying to tell. So I told Blake everything, right after that first kiss. Blake's ecstatic. He could not be more excited for me.

"Um . . ." Connor's a great guy and he's always super nice to me. The spark just isn't there. So maybe I could say that I just like him as a friend. Isn't that what I'd do if I weren't seeing Jason? "I, uh . . ." That sounds really bad, though. I don't want to hurt him. And he might not want to be friends with me after hearing that. "I can't. Go out with you."

Connor studies his moose towel.

"It's because . . ." I don't want him to get weird with me, so I have to tell him something. "Can you keep a secret?"

"Definitely," Connor says. "I'm really good at that."

"Okay, well . . . I'm seeing someone. But it's a secret, so you can't tell anyone."

"Who?"

"I can't tell you."

"I won't tell anyone."

"Yeah, but I still can't tell you."

Connor grins. "Is it someone scandalous?"

"Sort of." It feels so good to be talking about Jason even though Connor doesn't know who we're talking about. It's making me giddy. "Sorry I can't tell you."

"At least I wasn't rejected, eh?"

"You were *not* rejected."

"Of course you're taken. Why wouldn't you be?"

"You're sweet." I drop my water bottle into my bag and put on my flip-flops. "See you later?"

"You're coming back?"

"No, I mean . . . another day?"

"Oh. Yeah."

Walking by Jason's lifeguard chair, it's really hard not to say anything to him. I was planning on finding out about later tonight, but Connor's watching me. I don't want him to get suspicious. So I pass by Jason without even looking up.

29

The week before school starts flies by in a blur of Jason. We spend every second we can together. I'm not sneaking out at night anymore, though. I almost got caught coming back in the last time. It's seriously reducing our quality alone time. Plus, all these other things are going on.

MONDAY.

It's my last day helping Mom at the green market. We've just finished putting out the baskets of vegetables and setting up the price signs when someone goes, "Lani?"

I look up. And there's Jason's mom.

Oh, no. No no no no *no*.

These are two moms who were never supposed to meet. My

mom knows everyone so I'm sure she's met Jason's mom before, but I can tell that Mom can't quite remember who she is. As long as they were kept apart, neither of them could figure out how much time Jason and I have been spending together. Neither of them would conclude that we're more than friends. My mom's met Jason and his mom's met me, but they both think that whenever Jason and I do stuff, it's mostly a group situation.

The parental-gossip chain rivals their kids'. I can't risk the truth getting out that way.

"Hi," I say reluctantly. I consider hiding in the squash basket. It's probably not big enough. "Mom, do you know—"

"You're Jason's mom, right?" Mom extends her hand. They spend the next few minutes catching up on back-to-school news. I try to look busy even though we're done setting up. When a customer comes up to our table, I practically knock him over with enthusiasm. He buys some peppers.

Then I'm alone with the moms.

Who are staring at me.

"I was just saying how nice it is that you and Jason have become such good friends," Jason's mom goes.

"Oh, you've noticed that, too?" Mom asks, faux-innocently.

I am mortified.

"Well, I'd better be going," Jason's mom says. "I'm sure I'll see you again soon, Lani."

My face gets hot. Is it my imagination, or are the moms looking at me like they know something I wish they didn't know?

It's becoming increasingly obvious that I'm not fooling anyone.

TUESDAY.

Jason and I declare the night to be arts-and-crafts time. One of the kids at the pond brought Jason some extra kaleidoscope kits from his day camp, so we're making kaleidoscopes. I'm also putting Jason's perfect circle–drawing skills to work making some cardboard Earths for me to glue onto posters for One World.

After my parents met Jason, he was allowed in my room. With the door open. Yesterday I got the feeling that my parents have known exactly what Jason and I are the whole time I was telling them that we weren't. I'm still insisting we're just friends, though. Part of the whole arts-and-crafts night was so Jason could come over and show that nothing's going on.

We've spread out all the supplies on my bed. Jason is drawing yet another perfect circle.

"How can you always draw such perfect circles?" I go.

"It's an inherent skill. Circular sketching is one of those things that can't be developed."

"Fascinating."

The cardboard crunches as Jason cuts into it.

Out of nowhere, I'm like, "Did I ever tell you about the time Erin and I had our palms read?" I never told Jason that the psychic knew about him. But suddenly I have to tell him that she knew. With Erin coming home and school starting soon, I need to make sure things with us won't change.

"When was that?"

"Um . . . last April?"

"No, you never told me."

"Oh." I pick up one of Jason's cardboard circles. "Well, it was just . . . there's this psychic in town who reads palms and tarot cards and we went in." Some fibers are sticking out from the edge of the circle. I pull on them. "She knew about you. The psychic, I mean."

"Really?"

"Like, she didn't say *Jason* or anything, just that you were . . . that you were going to come into my life."

"Whoa."

"I know." I scrape my fingernail along the edge of the circle.

"How did you know she was talking about me?"

"It was obvious."

Jason takes the circle from me before I completely destroy it. "Did you want this to be a different shape, or . . . ?"

"Oh! Sorry."

"No worries. There are plenty more where that came from." Jason starts drawing another circle. "So . . . what did she say?"

"Just that you're . . . important to me."

I feel like I'm going to cry. It's really hard to find the right words when you're afraid to say the things you desperately want to say. I'm scared that things might change after our perfect summer is over. Underneath it all, the panic that Erin will eventually be back has always been there. Now it's suddenly like Erin will be home in a few days and I can't enjoy being with Jason the same way anymore. I'm all tense. The Unknown can attack at any time. It can rip your whole life to pieces. Things can change so quickly. I hate not knowing what's going to happen with us.

The uncertainty is killing me.

"Come here," Jason says.

I scrunch over a little.

"No," he goes. *"Here."*

I scrunch all the way over to him. I glance at my open door.

Jason puts his arms around me. I lean against him, feeling safe for now. I just wonder how much longer this feeling will last.

WEDNESDAY.

There have been a few days this summer that I thought were the hottest ever, but today is hotter than all of them put together. A walk on Venus would be a relief right about now. Jason has to work and I have the day off, so I asked Blake over to get soaked on the Slip 'n Slide. His internship just ended, but he's totally psyched to continue glassblowing. His mentor said he can use some of the studio space one day a week after school. He even wants to sell some of Blake's pieces. I'm really happy for him. He deserves good things.

When Blake comes out in his bathing suit, I whistle.

"Excuse me," I go, "no one told me this was a sexy party."

"Well, it must be if you were invited."

"Ha." I pick up the hose and blast it on the Slip 'n Slide. "Ready?"

"Wooo!" Blake takes a running leap and splats onto the Slip 'n Slide. "I call next turn!"

I love seeing Blake this way, like nothing bad has ever happened to him, like he has no worries. He's never this happy during the school year. I really hope being a senior will make his life more tolerable.

THURSDAY.

Blake wanted to check out some fish at the pet store, so I went with him. Every time he comes over, he's glued to my fish tank, adoring Wallace and Gromit. Blake wants to get an aquarium when he's at college. He would get one now if his house felt like home to him. He doesn't want to bring pets into a hostile environment.

The first thing we saw at the pet store was this scary white cat sitting on his own pedestal. He fluffed out his fur in a huff of attitude. His weird eyes were like lasers, way more expressive than human eyes. It felt like he could read my soul. His eyes were all, *Yeah. I know you. I know everything you're thinking.* The cat was acting all exotic and important. Which I guess is what happens when you're put on your own pedestal.

"He's freaking me out," I told Blake.

"Who?"

I pointed at the cat. The cat could totally tell I was pointing at him. His enormous blue eyes narrowed. *Yeah. I know what you've been doing all summer. I know you're sneaking around.*

All I wanted to do was leave, but I managed to get Phil a toy first. Then I ran out of there.

FRIDAY.

Jason has a surprise for me.

He's taking me somewhere secret. He won't tell me where. It's been like this for three days, with me asking for hints and him not giving me any. You'd think I'd be sick of playing this game by now, but I love it.

I also love being in Jason's room. It smells like him. All his stuff is here. His bed is really comfortable. I've confiscated it while Jason folds some laundry that his mom just brought up. Jason's house is always extra air-conditioned. I could seriously live here.

"Give me a hint," I say.

"No hints," Jason says.

"Just a little hint."

"Still no hints."

"Please?"

"I thought you liked surprises."

"I like them even more when I get a hint."

Phil's paws click toward us down the hall. He stands in the doorway, staring at me.

"Hey, Phil," I go.

Phil stares.

"You're such a pudding face. Pudding *face*!" I dangle my arm off the bed. Phil clicks over to me. He sniffs my hand. Then he waits to be petted.

I try a different approach with Jason. "Is it inside or outside?"

"It's both. No more hints."

Phil looks up at me with his sad, glassy eyes. I want to tell him that everything's going to be okay. He always seems so worried. And he's always snuffling his nose on the floor, like now. So I take out the toy I got for him at the pet store yesterday. That was such a freaky experience.

When I jingle the toy, Phil growls at it. Then he sneezes

and bites it and takes it over to the corner for some privacy.

"Ready?" Jason goes.

"For . . . I'm sorry, what is it we're doing again? I forget."

"Nice try."

We get in the Jeep and put on our sunglasses. The afternoon sunlight is incredibly bright. Since the road we're on really only leads to one place, I think I've finally figured out where we're going.

"Are we going to Smoke Rise?" I ask. That's where all the hot-air balloons come down. When Mom and I used to drive around following hot-air balloons, we always ended up there. I liked seeing the people who rode in those balloons. I always wondered what kind of people they were and if they ever got scared and what it's like to be that high up.

"Maybe," Jason says.

"What might we do at Smoke Rise?"

"Hmm. I haven't really thought about it."

When we get there, a hot-air balloon is coming down. We get out and watch it land. Every time a jet of flame is fired to heat the air inside the balloon, it makes a loud, harsh noise.

"This is so cool," I go. "How did you know when their balloon would be landing?"

"I didn't."

"Oh, so this is just a coincidence?"

"Exactly," he says. He holds my hand.

I scan the few other people here, but I don't see anyone from school. Not that I think any of them would be interested in something this dorky. You just never know who's going to be where.

Jason's like, "Let's go."

"Where?"

"To the surprise."

"I thought that *was* the surprise."

"What, that? No, that was just a balloon landing. You can see that anytime."

"So what's the surprise?"

Jason points to another balloon on the ground. Then he looks at me, all excited.

"What?" I go.

"Come on."

We go over to the balloon, which has rainbow stripes on it. There's a guy next to it, writing something on a clipboard. When he sees us he goes, "Hi there, Jason."

"Oh my god," I go. "Are you taking me for a hot-air-balloon ride?"

"If I said no, could I keep the surprise going?"

I've always wanted to go on a hot-air-balloon ride. And Jason knows it. He knows it and he didn't just sit around knowing it. He actually did something about it.

It's not until we're so high up with everything looking impossibly small below us that it hits me. The huge problems we deal with every day are actually really small. We're so focused on what bothers us that we don't even try to see our lives from a clearer perspective.

Everything will be okay. No matter what happens after Erin comes home, no matter how mad at me she gets, it will all work out the way it's supposed to. Isn't that what fate is all about? The

Energy influencing our actions, directing us toward our destiny? If Jason and I are destined to be together, then everything that happened this summer happened just the way it was supposed to.

Too bad Erin probably won't see it that way.

SATURDAY.

During a colossal lapse in judgment, I agreed to go in the pond.

Since that time we took the rowboat out on the lake, Jason's done a few more swimming lessons with me without any actual swimming involved. I hardly had to get in the water at all. One time I walked with him along the shore, getting my feet wet and looking for interesting shells. After a while I felt comfortable enough to go in up to my knees. It wasn't so bad. Last week we took the train a bunch of towns over to a public pool. Jason held me while I floated. I floated with my buddy in swimming, too, but I'm feeling like I can trust the water a little more now. I can't imagine ever trusting it completely, though.

But tonight, I'm excited about the water. Because tonight it's all about night swimming.

Green Pond is ours exclusively. If anyone catches us, Jason will use his lifeguarding status to justify trespassing. It's only 9:00, so I don't think we'll get in too much trouble if we're caught.

We linger at the edge of the pond, looking out at the vast darkness of it.

Jason holds my hand.

"Don't let go of me," he says.

"I'm never letting go of you." I'm so scared that I'm squeezing

Jason's hand way too hard. I can't help it. This will be my first time going into any water that's not a pool since the accident. Natural water is way scarier than pool water. Anything can happen out here.

The night is so clear. There are a million stars. I find the Big Dipper. It reassures me that I'll be safe.

We take a step. Then another.

I'm up to my ankles.

Then my knees.

Then my thighs.

When the water is up to my waist, I have to stop for a long time.

"This is as far as I can go," I decide.

"Are you sure?"

"I'm really sure."

"Well, let's just hang out here for a while and see what happens."

We talk about everything. Train-track walks and fate and horoscopes and our summer jobs and school and ideas for new note codes. When I eventually look back up at the stars, they're in different positions.

"Think you can go in a little more?" Jason says. "You're safe."

"I'll try."

I grasp his hand. We walk in farther. Soon, I'm up to my shoulders.

"You're doing great," he says. "I won't let anything happen to you."

Jason stands in front of me, holding my hands. "Would you let me pull you along for a few seconds? All you have to do is kick your feet behind you."

"For how many seconds?"

"Three?"

Can I really do this? As long as my feet are on the bottom of the pond, I know I probably won't drown. But once I can't feel the ground supporting me anymore . . .

Then I remember my goal. I want to swim in Hawaii next summer. I want to know what it feels like to be free.

"Okay," I go.

Jason looks surprised. "Really?"

"Hurry up before I change my mind."

It works. Jason pulls me along while I glide through the water for a few seconds, kicking behind me. We do it again and again until I'm not so scared anymore.

I've always hoped for this. When I would be strong enough to finally overcome my fear. When everything would begin to fall into place. My life finally has the chance to be everything I've always wanted it to be.

part three

september–october

"Fate is like a strange, unpopular restaurant,
filled with odd waiters who bring you things
you never asked for and don't always like."
——Lemony Snicket

"The expected is just the beginning. The un-
expected is what changes our lives."
——Meredith Grey

30

Sometimes things have to get worse before they can get better. I just never imagined that things could get this bad.

31

If you told me three months ago that Erin would ever think Jason is a loser, I would have been like no way. But here she is. Sitting on my front porch. Complaining about what a loser Jason is.

"Who breaks up with someone while they're away at camp?" Erin rants. "Who *does* that? In a *letter*?"

She's been home for two days. I haven't told her yet. Jason's the one who's going to tell her. He feels responsible. He had to go away for some family Labor Day–weekend thing, so he won't see Erin until school starts.

"Want more lemonade?" I ask.

"Totally," Erin goes. "This humidity is ridiculous."

I fill her glass with lemonade and add a twist of lime. I love adding a twist of lime. It's very adult.

I was really hoping that Erin would still be swooning over her summer fling with Lee. It's not like that, though. I've never seen her this angry. She's been ranting about Jason since she got here. Plus, she ranted the whole time when I saw her yesterday. She's nowhere near finished.

Facing reality is a major buzz kill.

"It would be one thing if I saw it coming," Erin rants on. "Like if we were fighting or something. But everything was fine when I left. How could that have changed so quickly? I wasn't even here!"

I nod sympathetically. Hiding the truth from her is killing me. Actually, her extreme anger is making me scared to tell her, so I'm kind of relieved that Jason's doing it instead.

"What do you think happened?" she goes.

"Oh . . . um . . ."

"Where does he get off dumping me in a freaking letter? Who the eff does he think he is?!" Erin's glass jerks. Lemonade sloshes onto the porch floor.

"Sorry," she says.

"That's okay." Maybe this would be a good time to focus the conversation on Lee. I go, "Where's Lee from again?"

"Somewhere down the shore."

"Is he coming up?"

"Maybe."

"That's cool."

A mourning dove hoos.

Erin doesn't say anything else about Lee.

"I can't believe I have to face everyone at school," she says.

"Don't worry. No one knows."

"Oh, they will. The rumors will be rampant. What I am supposed to say when they ask why we aren't together anymore? Everyone will find out that Jason dumped me." Erin's eyes get watery. "I've never been so humiliated in my life."

"Don't worry. No one has to know. It's not like Jason's going to tell anyone."

"How do you know?"

"He's not like that."

"Good one," Erin scoffs. "I didn't think he would break up with me in a freaking letter, either. But there you go. Who knows what else that dumbass is capable of?"

As soon as she leaves, I call Jason. I tell him I can't see him again until Erin knows about us. Being with him this summer when it was just the two of us was one thing. Now that Erin's back, I can't face her if I'm still hooking up with Jason. I feel like the most horrible person ever. It's hard enough seeing her and acting like nothing's changed. Like, what, Erin will come over after school and then I'll go sneak around with Jason after?

What the hell was I *thinking*?

Jason's like, "What are you saying?"

"It's different now that she's back. I can't see you and then pretend like nothing's going on. It's not fair to her."

"Are you saying we can't see each other at all? Or just at school?"

"At all."

"Until she knows."

"Right."

"What about after she knows?"

"Then we won't have to hide it anymore."

I grab Magic 8 Ball and shake it. I think my question: *Is Erin going to be okay?* Magic 8 Ball says, SIGNS POINT TO YES.

"Look." I hear Jason switch the phone to his other ear. "You know I want to tell her in person. I can see if she'll get together when I get home tomorrow."

"Are you going over to her house?"

"I was thinking more like meeting her at The Fountain."

I don't say anything. How can he take her there? That's our place.

"Lani?"

"I'm here."

"What's wrong?"

"Why do you have to go there?"

"We don't have to go anywhere."

"But you said you wanted to tell her in person."

"I do. So where do you think we should go?"

It really shouldn't matter. Jason can tell her at The Fountain if he wants. It's just that I don't want the image of Jason telling Erin that we're together to be there every time I go in for some gelato.

Why am I being so crazy about this?

"No, it's okay," I tell him. "Go to The Fountain."

"I haven't even asked her to meet up yet. She might say no."

"Then what?"

"Then I'll have to tell her at school."

"But that's two whole days from now."

"Okay, I'll call and ask if she'll meet tomorrow night."

"Are you sure you're okay with telling her? Because I can—"

"Yes. It has to be me."

After we hang up, all these annoying What If questions come rushing in. What if Erin wants Jason back? And she tells him that? And he feels bad and gets back together with her? What if he can't tell her the truth about us?

When the phone rings, I jump. It's Jason already.

"That was fast," I go.

"She hung up on me."

"What?"

"Yeah. I couldn't even ask her."

"What did she say?"

"Nothing. When she heard it was me, she hung up."

"Did you try calling back?"

"So she could hang up on me again? I don't think so."

"So now what?"

"I could try texting her. But I doubt she'll want to see me."

"Just tell her you have to talk to her. Say it's really important."

"She'll want to know why."

"Then I guess we have to wait until school."

This is so messed up. I just told Jason that we shouldn't see each other until Erin knows. There's no way I'm waiting two more days to see him again. Except there's not much I can do about it. It's not like I can tell Erin that Jason wants to talk. She'll want to know what for. And I can't tell her about us because Jason is insisting that it has to be him.

"Well . . ." Jason goes, "I guess I'll see you at school."

"Yeah. See you there."

Two days is forever from now. I don't know how I'm going to survive until then. All I can think about is how good it feels when we're together. Just being with him and kissing him and knowing that nothing can get in the way of us.

Except maybe reality.

32

Today is the worst first day of school ever.

Forget that Erin refused to talk to Jason when he went up to her. Forget that she still doesn't know.

There's a rumor going around that Blake is gay.

I never thought this would happen. I have no idea how it got started. If people were going to spread that around, wouldn't it have been out there a long time ago? Who's all of a sudden going to start a rumor like this senior year?

It's not like Blake's done anything different recently to make someone suddenly notice him. He was totally low-key all summer, spending most of his time at glassblowing.

Nothing about him has changed.

I'm the only person who knows he's gay and there's no way I would tell anyone. Blake knows he can trust me with—

Wait.

There was that day at the end of last year with Jason. When I blurted out about Blake being gay. Jason promised he wouldn't tell anyone. And I believed him. I still do.

But if he didn't tell anyone, who did?

Jason and I have physics together second period. We're getting assigned seats tomorrow, but for today we can sit wherever we want. I snagged us two desks next to each other in the back. We need to talk.

When Jason comes in, I wave to him. He doesn't smile when he sees me, like I thought he would. That's okay, though. I'm not smiling, either.

Jason sits down. He goes, "Did you hear about Blake?"

"Of course. The whole school's talking about it." I'm trying not to be mad, but this is ridiculous. Jason is the only other person who knows about Blake. How else could this have gotten out?

The bell rings. Everyone shuts up. After our teacher hands out the class contract and starts going over it, I quietly pop my binder open. I take out a piece of paper.

I write:

How do people know about Blake?

I fold the note and pass it to Jason.

He writes back:

I have no idea.

Then:

We're the only people who know. Or, we _were_.

What are you saying?

Did you tell anyone about Blake?

Of course not! I can't believe you're even asking me that.

Then how else did it get out?

It wasn't me. I swear.

I glance over at Jason. I think he's telling the truth. Why would he tell anyone anyway? That's just not something he would do.

After class, Blake finds me in the hall. With all the first-day-back chaos, Blake's able to pull me out the side doors without any adult types seeing.

He goes, "Did you tell someone?"

"No!"

Blake doesn't look convinced. "Are you sure?"

"Why would I do that to you?"

"I don't know, Lani. That's what I'm trying to figure out."

"I didn't tell anyone."

"Then how does everyone know?"

I want to believe Jason. I mean, I do believe him. I just had to ask if he told. He was obviously offended that I didn't completely trust him, but no one else freaking *knows*.

Blake puts his face really close to mine. "Swear to me on my life that you didn't tell anyone."

I can't swear on his life. That would totally be challenging fate. If things are ever going to be okay, I have to tell the truth. Starting now.

"Promise you won't get mad if I tell you," I say.

"Tell me what?"

"Promise you won't get mad first."

"I can't promise that."

"I told Jason."

"What the—"

"I didn't mean to! It just came out!"

"How does something like that just come out? You promised me you'd never tell anyone!"

"He was saying that he thought you were my boyfriend and I—"

"So you told him I'm gay? You couldn't just say we're friends?"

"But he said—"

"It doesn't matter what he said! My life is over! Do you even get that?"

I've never seen Blake this furious. Not even after the worst fights with his dad.

My eyes tear up. "I'm sorry. It just came out!"

Blake is disgusted with me. "I trusted you," he says.

"You can still trust me. Just let me explain. He—"

"Save it," Blake says. He turns away.

"Wait, let me—"

"Nothing you say can fix this. Everyone knows. Because of you."

Blake storms off, away from school.

I chase after him across the lawn. Trying to keep up with Blake is hard. He's way taller than me. He's walking so fast that I have to run to keep up with him.

I try to explain again. "Please just—"

"How could you do this to me?"

"Jason said he wouldn't tell anyone."

"And look how well that turned out!"

"I don't think he's the one who told."

"You told more people?!"

"No!"

"Then who else would tell, Lani? You're the only one who knew!"

"I don't know. But it wasn't Jason. I just asked him about it in physics and I could tell it wasn't him."

He stops walking. "Okay, think. Where were you guys when you told him?"

"Here."

"At *school?*"

"No one else was in the room with us—"

"You were in a classroom?"

I nod.

"Which one?"

"Um." I can't remember. It was cloudy. The room was dark. Jason—

"Which *one*?"

"The one next to guidance. One seventeen."

"And no one else was in there with you?"

"No."

"Are you sure?"

"Yes."

"Did you check everywhere?"

I didn't. I mean, you go into an empty classroom, it's dark, you don't see anyone sitting there, you assume it's empty.

"Whatever," Blake says.

This time when he leaves, I let him go. If I were Blake, I'm sure I'd be leaving, too. Some of these kids can be brutal. I can't believe that homophobia still exists. It should be an archaic concept by now. Why can't everyone understand that we're all human— different but the same?

33

Blake never came back to school yesterday. Which is really bad, considering it was the first day and all. He has to be here today.

While I'm waiting for Blake out front, Jason pulls into the student lot. I watch him park his Jeep. I wish we could just be together. I've never wanted anything so much in my life.

Jason walks toward me across the lawn. He tried talking to Erin again after school yesterday. She ignored him. Then he tried calling her last night. She didn't pick up. The same thing happened with me trying to call Blake an embarrassing amount of times.

"Why don't I just tell her?" I said when Jason called me. "She's obviously not going to talk to you. We can't keep waiting like this."

"I'm not waiting," Jason went. "I'm ready to tell her."

"What about emailing her?"

"It's not right to do this over email."

"It's not right that we can't be together, either."

Watching him coming closer, every part of me aches to touch him. But then everyone would totally see.

Unless . . .

Jason walks by slowly, all close. He looks at me. He doesn't say anything. His eyes are the darkest green.

I go, "Meet me under the stairs in the science wing before lunch." We have the same lunch again this year. Except this time, Erin's also in our lunch. It was really hard to sit with her yesterday, pretending nothing was wrong while I snuck looks at Jason three tables over. I hope he snuck looks at me, too. As if that didn't suck enough, we're not allowed to leave for lunch this year. Some idiotic senior ruined lunch privileges at the end of last year by making a total ruckus in Blimpie, so now we're being punished. Seniors are trapped in the caf until next semester.

Jason nods and keeps walking. I know I said that I didn't want to see him until Erin knows, but I can't do this anymore. He's all I can think about. Now that we can't be together, I want him a hundred times more. It's driving me crazy.

Blake finally shows up two minutes before the first bell. He isn't exactly rushing to be on time.

"Please don't stay mad at me," I go. "I hate that we're in a fight."

Blake's like, "Whose fault is that, I wonder?" Then he brushes past me.

Every class before lunch takes forever to end. Glaring at the clock in history, I swear time actually goes backward.

As soon as the bell rings, I shove my stuff in my bag and run to the science wing. There's a secret hiding place under the stairs. I don't know if anyone else knows about it. I found it one day in ninth grade when we were doing an activity in the hall for bio and my Styrofoam ball rolled under there.

Waiting for Jason, I concentrate on being quiet. If someone found me hiding under the stairs like this, I would be mortified. I don't know what I'm going to do when he gets here. I just know that I have to be alone with him.

I hear the door at the top of the stairs open. Some girls are laughing.

"It's just a nasty rumor," one girl says. "He's not gay."

"How would you know?" the other girl fires back.

"Um, maybe because he had a major crush on me last year?"

"Did he ask you out?"

"Not exactly. But he totally flirted with me in chemistry."

"That doesn't prove anything."

"Why would he flirt with me if he's gay?"

"Hello! So no one would suspect him?"

"Not like it matters. He was going out with Lani."

I hold my breath. Who are these girls? I don't recognize their voices. Do I know them? And why aren't they moving?

"Maybe they're just friends."

"Yeah, right! Have you ever seen them together?"

"Yeah, but—"

"Trust me. Nothing about that is platonic."

The door swings open again. A new girl is like, "Where'd you guys go?" Her voice is lower than the others'.

"Here, obviously."

"Isn't Blake going out with Lani?" the first girl goes.

"Blake's gay." This from the girl who just got here.

"No, he's not. He totally flirted with me last year."

"What a load," the new girl says. "Ryan said he heard Lani say that Blake is gay."

"Which Ryan?"

"Ryan Campanelli."

"When?"

"At the end of last year."

"Yeah, like she'd really be talking about that in front of Ryan."

"No, he was in the other room. You know how you can hear everything from one seventeen in the guidance office waiting room?"

"Oh, right. It has that weird vent thing."

"Same with two forty-two and two forty-four. I had Communications in two forty-two last year and you could totally hear everything from two forty-four."

"So Ryan was going in to see Mr. Bradley when he heard Lani. She was like—"

The door swings open. "Where are you girls supposed to be?" a Teacher Voice says. "Let's go."

I hear the girls shuffle off. I'm dying to see who they are, but there's no way I'm risking exposure.

Jason was supposed to be here ten minutes ago.

A few seconds later, the door bangs open. Jason comes running down the stairs. I know it's him without looking.

"Sorry about that," Jason says. He bends down and ducks under the stairwell. "Those girls took forever to leave. I was—"

I kiss him.

Jason goes, "I miss you."

"Same here."

"I'm going to email Erin."

"But you said—"

"I know. But she's not giving me a choice."

I kiss him some more.

"How's Blake doing?" he whispers.

"Dude!" I whisper-yell. "I just found out who told about Blake. It was Ryan!"

"Ryan Campanelli?"

"Yes! He was in guidance when we were in one seventeen. He heard me telling you about Blake."

"How?"

"You can hear everything from one seventeen in the guidance waiting room through the vents."

"Oh, crap."

"I can't believe he waited so long to say something."

"At least now we know who did. And you know that I didn't."

"I knew you—"

I don't get to finish what I was saying. Because Jason is kissing me. And nothing else matters.

34

When Jason calls me later to let me know that he finally emailed Erin, I'm relieved. He forwards me the email so I can see what he said. It's all about how he never meant to hurt her but he wants to be with me.

I have no idea what Erin's going to do. Well, I sort of have an idea. A scary idea.

I think about calling her. I keep picking up my phone and putting it back down. Of course she's going to be mad. Of course she's going to hate me. There's nothing I can do about it. All I can do is wait for her to talk to me again.

Maybe she never will. Blake still won't talk to me. I've tried calling him a bunch more times, but he keeps screening. It's like he dropped right out of my life over one stupid mistake.

When the phone rings three hours later, I can't believe it's Erin.

"Hey," I go.

"Hey," she goes back.

No one says anything. There's a hollow humming noise.

Erin's like, "How's it going?"

"Okay . . ."

"How's Blake doing?"

"He's . . . not good."

"I'm sure."

Erin doesn't sound mad. I was totally expecting Erin to be mad. Maybe she didn't read Jason's email yet.

"Know what I heard?" Erin says.

"What?"

"You were the one who outed Blake."

"No, it was Ryan Campanelli!"

"I heard it was you, and Ryan was just telling people what you said."

"I only told Jason! No one else was there!"

"Oh, you were alone with Jason?"

"No, we weren't, like, *alone*, just in a classroom alone."

"Why?"

"Um . . . I don't really remember."

"Do you remember lying to my face?"

My heart skips a beat.

I go, "Did you get Jason's email?"

"I want to hear you say it."

"Say what?"

"That you're a lying bitch who stole my boyfriend."

My heart stops beating entirely.

"He's not your boyfriend anymore," I say, my voice all shaky.

"Oh, yeah. Thanks for reminding me."

"I didn't mean—"

"You know, I had a bad feeling when I was getting on the camp bus. I almost said something. But I *trusted* you. Bianca kept saying how you were flirting with Jason at lunch, but I always defended you. I should have known. Why else would you guys go off together to some private table like that?"

"We weren't flirting. And you were fine with us sitting together."

"I can't believe I told you to hang out with Jason while I was away!"

"Just read his email."

"I already did. And now the whole class can read it."

"What do you mean?"

"I forwarded it to everyone. They should really know how you are. Like how you stole my boyfriend and lied about it to my face. *So* not cool."

Fear spikes through me. I knew Erin would be mad, but this is outrageous. She forwarded Jason's email to the whole class? It's like I don't even know her anymore. What kind of person would do something like that?

Someone whose life I ruined.

Someone who wants to ruin mine back.

Erin's like, "And after everything I've done for you. You wouldn't even be here if it wasn't for me."

Harsh. She's never brought up the accident like that. I mean, we've talked about it and of course I've thanked Erin for keeping me alive, but she's never said anything that brutal to me before.

She's right, though. Erin means more to me than anyone else. I can't believe I let things go this far.

"I'm really, really sorry," I tell her. "I'll do anything to make this right."

"Anything?"

"Yeah."

"Then stop seeing Jason."

How was this supposed to go again? Jason was going to tell Erin about us, she'd get mad, but then Jason and I would be together and eventually she'd get over it. This is turning out all wrong. Or maybe not. Maybe this is the Energy's way of reminding me about everything I'd lose if Erin weren't in my life. I wouldn't just be losing a friend. I'd be losing a part of my history, someone who's like a sister to me.

I've already hurt Erin enough. If she had to watch Jason and me together, it would be torture for her.

"Fine," I say. "I won't see him anymore. I won't even talk to him."

"Promise?"

"I promise."

"I'll try to believe you. Not that it'll change what you did."

"Erin, it's over. I won't even look at him."

"That's the least you can do."

"I'm so sorry."

"That's nice. Too bad no one cares. Anyway, have fun at school tomorrow. It should be *really* fun for you."

35

Everyone knows.

You know how you can tell when people are talking about you? Especially people who used to be your friends? It's like that. Everyone thinks I'm an evil boyfriend-stealer who goes around wrecking her best friend's life.

None of them knows the truth. And there's no way to tell them that Erin's lying.

Going to my locker before homeroom is supreme misery. People stare at me. Others turn away when I look at them. Some of them laugh. A girl I don't even know bumps me. Hard.

Everyone hates me.

Before Erin forwarded Jason's email to the whole world, she wrote at the top of it how I planned the whole thing. She wrote how I wanted Jason all along and totally stole him right out from under her. She even changed his email to make us look worse and her look better. Of course everyone believes her. She's so convincing even *I* almost believe her.

I get to my locker and focus on my lock combination. I don't want to look at anyone else. I can't stand seeing that much hate in people's eyes.

When Danielle comes up to me, I could not be more relieved. It was starting to feel like I had zero friends left.

I'm all, "Hey, did you get a chance to read that article?" We have our first One World meeting of the year in a few days. She's helping me with a presentation for new members.

"Yeah . . . um . . ." Danielle takes the article out of her bag. The edge is all crumpled. She gives it to me. "I can't really help you with this."

"Why not?"

"I just . . ." She looks around. A bunch of people are watching us. ". . . can't." Then she practically runs away from me.

Fabulous. Even my friends hate me now. Erin's email torment can't be why Danielle just bailed on me, though. As if she'd believe any of that without even talking to me. I have to find out what's wrong with her.

The day just gets worse from there. It's like no one's giving me the chance to tell my side. Everyone's just assuming I don't have one. Even people I don't know. Like when I'm answering a question in physics, two girls start whispering. I don't have to hear what they're saying to know they're whispering about me.

It's really hard to be in this class with Jason and not talk to him. Or even look at him. We have assigned seats now. He's far

away. I resist sneaking looks at him to see if he's sneaking looks
at me.

After I got off the phone with Erin last night, I called Jason to
tell him about my promise to her. It was one of the most depress-
ing conversations ever.

As if physics wasn't awkward enough, lunch is even worse.
After I get my lunch, I just stand there with my tray, searching for
a safety net.

Erin's sitting with some of the Golden Kids, including Bianca.
They're all listening to what I'm sure is a livid rant about how evil
I am. Bianca gives me a nasty glare. I knew she was spying on me
and Jason last year. I just didn't know she was low enough to go
blabbing all of her distortions to Erin.

Blake's sitting with some art geeks. He looks so sad. All he has
in front of him is a ginger ale. His manorexic tendencies escalate
in times of stress.

Jason's on the other side of the caf. I recognize some of the
people he's sitting with from mentoring. I'm not sure if he saw
me yet. I wish I could go over there and sit with him. I just want
things to be like they were this summer.

Of course that's impossible.

I feel really bad for him. It's obvious why the Golden Kids are
taking Erin's side.

Jason's the one who lied to them.

Jason's the one who dumped Erin in a letter.

Jason's the one who avoided them all summer to be with me.

But none of those things was Jason's fault. None of this would
be happening if I hadn't let Jason kiss me that first time.

There's an empty table in the far corner. It's the only safe place to sit. On my way over, I pass a table with some empty seats. One girl looks at me like she dares me to sit there. Then she drops her bag in the free chair next to her to make sure I don't.

I sit at the empty table. I try to look like I don't care that I'm all alone. Or that everyone in here is talking about me. Maybe things aren't as bad as I think. It's really just the Golden Circle that hates me. Not necessarily the whole school. But they're a huge group. And there are enough other people who think I'm a boyfriend-stealing slut that it totally feels like the whole school hates me.

People stare.

I shake my juice.

People stare some more.

The cap is impossible to twist open.

It's really hard to not cry.

The cap suddenly twists off. I scrape my hand on the edge of the table. I'm bleeding. I could go to the nurse. But then I'd have to walk out with everyone staring at me even more. I just can't deal with that. So I press a napkin against my hand and wait for the bleeding to stop.

No one comes over to sit with me.

After staring at the table for a long time, I try ripping open my bag of mixed nuts. It won't rip. My eyes are all watery. I tell myself to calm down, that everything will be okay. But myself is just like, *That's such a lie.*

I press my tourmalinated quartz. It's hopeless. An entire bucket of tourmalinated quartz couldn't balance me.

I look over at Jason. He quickly looks away. Now he's avoiding eye contact.

My bag of mixed nuts finally opens. I try chewing a cashew. It tastes like cardboard.

I've never felt so alone in my entire life.

It's just so tragic. All of us sitting at different tables. Hating each other. I wish I knew how to fix it.

Jason gets up.

My pulse races. Is he coming over here?

Jason shuffles away to clear his tray. I watch him crush his grape soda can. He puts all of his recyclables into the bins, separating them carefully from the garbage. There's something sad about the way he does this slowly, like he's completely exhausted. Clearly, recycling is his routine now. It's like he's not even thinking about it.

He's changed. Because of me.

When he's done, Jason turns around and catches me watching him. He still doesn't come over. He just goes back to his table.

Bianca comes over to me. She's like, "Erin wanted me to tell you she wants her red bag back."

"What?"

"You know. Her red bag? The one she let you borrow like two months ago that you never gave back?"

Is this girl for real? Did Erin seriously send her over like we're in some sixth-grade fight? How lame is that?

I go, "Seriously?"

"Um, yeah."

"Well, you can tell Erin that she has tons of stuff she's borrowed from me and I want it all back first."

"I'll give her the message. Oh, and just so you know? People are finally telling Erin what they really think of you."

"Which people?"

"Everyone. More specifically, everyone you decided wasn't good enough to be your friends."

How can anyone still be pissed about that? It wasn't like I made an official announcement that the entire Golden Circle sucks. I just gradually drifted away from them. Bianca's acting like no one's allowed to grow apart from anyone else. Which is incredibly stupid.

"They're really mad at you," Bianca adds.

"What am I supposed to do about it?"

"Nothing. I just thought you should know."

"Thanks for that."

"They've been mad at you for a while, but this just makes it worse. We all assumed you and Erin would be BFF forever, so we kept our mouths shut about you. But now she deserves to know the truth."

"Forever is redundant."

"Hm?"

"You don't need to say *forever* after *BFF*. The last *F* stands for *forever*."

Bianca whips back around and prances off.

I didn't get why Erin is still friends with Bianca, but now it's clear. They've been friends for so long, that's just the way it's always been. Even though Bianca has changed into someone pathetic, Erin still sees her as her friend Bianca. She doesn't see who Bianca really is now. Erin's just clinging to the memory of who she used to be.

I can't stay here. I have to leave *now*.

Unfortunately, you're not allowed to leave during the last ten minutes of lunch. Something about the adults being afraid that if they let us out too soon, the halls would get all crowded with kids loitering. Why didn't I think of this before? I could have gotten a bathroom pass and forgotten to come back.

The only way to convince the monitor to let me out is to make him believe I have an emergency. That always works in class. Especially when there's a sub. You just say it's an emergency and the teacher has to let you go. Even though it's probably not an emergency. Because if it actually is one and the teacher doesn't let you go, they could get in a lot of trouble. Like if you were sick and they didn't let you go and you threw up in class, it would be the teacher's fault. None of them wants that kind of potential trouble. It's particularly effective when the teacher's a guy and you're a girl. No guy teacher wants to hear about anything related to female issues.

A billion eyes follow my progress toward the door.

I approach the monitor. He's one of the older teachers.

"Can I help you?" he says in this tone like there's no way I'm going anywhere so why am I even trying.

"May I please use the bathroom?"

He consults his watch. "Eight minutes left of lunch. You can go then."

"But I have to go now."

"Sorry. Can't help you."

"Please. I really have to go."

One of the girls at the table next to Erin's has been listening the whole time. She yells, "Yeah. Lani *really* has to use the bathroom. She has diarrhea something *fierce.*"

Everyone on this side of the cafeteria cracks up. My face turns bright red.

Although it isn't a female issue, this teacher clearly does not want to deal with my situation. So he isn't about to argue that I don't have to go.

He waves me out. "Go ahead," he says.

I smack the door open and run for it.

The rest of the day is excruciating. Mom picks me up, since I'm not about to get a ride home from Erin. I almost ask her to drop me off at Danielle's, but I decide it's better to ride my bike over later so I'll have a way to leave quickly if I have to. Going over to her house will be the best way to find out what's going on with her. She probably won't pick up if I call her, and I really need to know why she's mad at me. So after dinner, I ride my bike to Danielle's.

She opens the door. Then she just stands there.

"Can I come in?" I go.

Danielle's all, "Why are you here?"

"Because I want to know what's wrong."

"Same thing that's bothering everyone else, I guess."

"What, that I'm some evil boyfriend-stealer? You seriously believe that?"

Danielle glances over her shoulder. "I can't really have anyone over right now," she says.

"I'm not leaving until you tell me what's wrong."

She comes out, closing the door behind her. She crosses her arms.

"Well?" I go. "Why are you mad?"

"Erin told me what you said."

"Which is . . . ?"

"She said you didn't want to invite me to your birthday party."

"I never said that!"

"What happened to spending your birthday alone? You said no one was coming over."

"It was only three people. It was nothing."

"If it was so nothing, then why did you lie?"

"I'm sorry. I didn't know what else to do."

"You could have invited me."

"I was going to! Erin was the one who said not to."

"And you listened to her? How come she got to go and I didn't?"

"It wasn't even a party! We were just hanging out!"

"So what, I'm not good enough to hang out with you guys?"

"No! I mean, yes, of course you are. I just didn't think you'd want to, is all."

"Why wouldn't I?"

I can't really admit that Erin and Danielle wouldn't get along. Erin's always resented my friendship with Danielle. Danielle would have been fine with coming over, but Erin would have had a problem with it. The whole night would have been awkward.

"Do you even know Erin?" I say. "Or Blake? What would we have talked about?"

"That's not the point. Why didn't you defend me when Erin said not to invite me? Aren't we good friends, too?"

"You know we are. I just . . . the whole thing was stupid. I should have asked you over. I'm sorry I didn't."

"Yeah. Me, too."

"So . . . are we friends again?"

"Not so much."

"Danielle, I'm really sorry I didn't—"

"It's not just about your birthday. You lied to me when I asked you if anything was going on with Jason."

"What makes you think something was?"

"Were you at school today?"

"You're just going to believe some rumor without even asking me if it's true?"

"Is it?"

There's no point in hiding the truth anymore. "It didn't happen the way Erin said."

"I can't believe you didn't tell me. Why didn't you trust me?"

"It's not that I didn't trust you. I just couldn't talk about it. With anyone."

"Even Blake?"

Crap. With Blake being mad at me, he could have told Danielle that he knew about Jason all along. I can't risk any more lies.

"I told him," I admit. "But he kind of already knew."

"Why didn't you tell *me*?"

I shake my head. It's impossible to answer this in a way that won't offend her. Danielle and I are close. I'm sure she wouldn't have told anyone. It's just that Blake and I are closer. I know for sure that I can trust him with anything.

Apparently, there are varying degrees of trust.

"I have to go," Danielle says. She opens her door.

"Wait, can we—"

There's no chance to finish what I want to say. Unless I feel like talking to a door that was just shut in my face.

36

Some things that suck:

- My eyes are in a permanent state of redness from crying all weekend.
- Blake still won't talk to me.
- Neither will Erin.
- Or Danielle.
- I can't eat without feeling like I'm immediately going to throw up.
- Jason and I will never be together.

Sleeping is always good. While you're sleeping, you don't have to think about how miserable your life is. But then you wake up and there it is all over again. Your miserable life.

I don't want to get up. I don't want to go to school.

I get up and go to school anyway.

As soon as I get there, I know I should have stayed home.

There's a bunch of kids crowded around some lockers, talking and laughing. They all have those big eyes people get when something's happening. I push through them to find out what everyone's looking at.

They're looking at Blake's locker.

Which says HOMO in big, yellow, spray-painted letters.

I can't believe someone actually did this. People are so hurtful it breaks my heart. Why can't they just leave him alone?

The crowd opens up a little. Blake comes through.

Everyone stops talking.

No one says anything to him. They just watch to see what he'll do.

You'd never know that Blake just saw what his locker says. He turns the dial of his lock slowly, focusing on the numbers. Trying to pretend that everything is normal so no one will see his pain.

Everyone keeps staring. They're watching Blake like he's some kind of zoo animal. No one's doing anything to defend him.

I go over to Blake and stand in front of him, facing the crowd.

"What's with you guys?" I say. "Don't you have anything better to do?"

Blake opens his locker. He takes books out.

"If you want to talk about me, go ahead. But leave Blake alone."

No one goes away.

"Leave!" I yell.

Mr. Bradley comes over. He's all, "What's going on here?" Blake's locker is open, so he doesn't see what it says. "Homeroom!" he yells. "Let's go!"

The crowd breaks up. A few kids linger behind, determined to see Blake crack.

Blake shuts his locker. He stares at the spray paint.

"I can help you get that off," I say.

"It won't come off."

"Yeah, it will. I can borrow that industrial cleaner the janitors use to get graffiti off the desks." The janitors love me. I make their lives easier with all of the recycling stuff One World does. They totally let me borrow whatever I want.

"You think it'll work?" Blake says.

"Absolutely. I'll go get it."

"Wait." Blake hugs me. "Thanks."

The kids who were still watching leave, disappointed that the emotional meltdown they were hoping for didn't happen. Blake's stronger than they'll ever know. He'll never show them how much he really hurts.

I was hoping that Blake and I would make up after we cleaned his locker. We didn't talk as we scrubbed at the spray paint. But after, he just said thanks again and went to class.

Connor's like the only one still being nice to me. He always walks with me if we're switching between classes in the same direction. We either talk or IM every night. He's so worried about me. Which is sweet, but I don't want to give him the wrong idea.

What if he thinks that since things apparently didn't work out with Jason, there's a chance I'd go out with him? I'm hoping he can tell that I just want to be friends.

When Connor said he'd come over tonight, I jumped at the chance for some company. Ostracism is a lonely place.

Peering into my closet, we try to decide on a game. I seriously need some mindless escape time.

"How about cards?" Connor says.

"Do you know how to play 500?"

"You need at least four people for that."

"No you don't."

"Of course you do. If we're the only team, then who would we play against?"

"Huh?"

"You're talking about the French Canadian 500, right?"

"No, Rummy 500. There's more than one 500?"

"It would appear so."

"Outrageous."

"We could try some art therapy. That always works for me."

"Does this mean you don't want to play Clue?"

"Would you rather play Clue or make Oobleck?"

"Oobleck!"

"Do you have any cornstarch?"

"I think so. . . ."

We spend the next hour regressing back to a time before everything got so complicated.

"Feeling any better?" Connor asks.

"Yes and no. I mean, this totally helps take my mind off things, but then it's like all of a sudden I'll remember and everything sucks again."

"It must be really hard for you. Especially with the accident and everything."

"How do you know about that?"

"Someone told me."

"When?"

"Last year."

"Someone just randomly told you?"

"Not exactly." Connor squeezes some Oobleck. It changes from a liquid into a solid. "There was this one time in art when you were leaning over a painting and I could see under your bangs a little. I saw part of your scar, so I asked a friend if they knew how you got it."

"Oh."

"Is that why you never go swimming at the pond?"

"Yeah."

"Sorry, we don't have to talk about this. It's not—"

"No, it's fine. I feel like talking."

I tell Connor everything. It feels good to talk to someone I can trust who's not directly involved. I'm just thankful that there's still someone left to listen.

37

"Thanks for coming out, everybody," I say. "Let's go over who we are and what we do."

The first meeting of One World is always exciting. Our club gets bigger every year. You never know who's going to join. Some people can surprise you.

And then there are the ones who will never change.

Bianca and Marnie keep laughing. Every time I start talking, they laugh.

"Is something funny?" I ask Bianca.

She goes, "Definitely."

Then they burst out laughing again.

I continue the orientation. "I've been a member of One World since ninth grade. As president, it's my job to let you know about

community events, like park cleanups and educational out-
reach."

Marnie raises her hand.

"Marnie?" I go.

"Yeah, I was just wondering if you'll also let us know about
upcoming workshops."

"Like what kind of workshops?"

"Oh, I don't know . . . maybe one on how to steal your best
friend's boyfriend?"

Some other girls laugh and whisper. None of them is on my
side except for Sophie, who just joined. Danielle won't even look
at me. The boys (all two of them) awkwardly shuffle their feet.

"Maybe," I say, "but I don't think you should sign up for that
one. No guy would ever want you, no matter how many workshops you took."

The boys snicker. Everyone's gaping at Marnie, waiting to see
what she'll do.

Marnie goes, "At least I'm not a slut."

"Shut up, Marnie," Sophie says.

I go back to explaining about the club and what our goals for
the year are. At least Sophie's not evil. Too bad she's not in my
lunch. Not like I have an appetite anymore. I should just avoid the
cafeteria all together. Maybe I'll eat lunch under the stairs from
now on.

I'm still not hungry later that night when Mom yells that dinner's ready, but there's no way I can avoid her. If I don't go down
to dinner, I'll have to endure an endless barrage of questions I

don't want to answer. So after I feed Wallace and Gromit, I go downstairs.

My parents know something's wrong. There's a lot of nervous chitchat about nothing.

"Don't these tomatoes look incredible?" Mom gushes.

"Incredible," Dad confirms.

"I just picked them."

"Guess the garden's winding down."

They glance at me. Then they exchange a look across the table. They think I'm not aware of the look, but I can sense it.

I stare at my plate, scraping my fork against it, pushing the potatoes around.

"Honey, you haven't touched your dinner," Mom says.

"I'm touching it," I tell her. "I'm just not eating it."

"Are you feeling okay?"

"I'm fine."

"You have to eat," Dad says.

"I'm not hungry. I had a really big lunch."

They exchange another look. I'm sure they know I'm lying. When you're as little as I am, losing even two pounds makes a difference. I've probably lost more than that since school started.

Mom's like, "You know you can talk to us. About anything."

"I know."

"Or . . . I can take you to the health center if you want to . . . discuss this with a specialist."

"What kind of specialist?"

They do their look again.

I go, "Will you guys stop looking at each other and tell me what's going on?"

Dad's not touching this one. He stabs another tomato slice.

"You haven't been eating," Mom goes. "We're concerned."

"Is that what—you think I'm anorexic or something?"

"You're too thin."

"I don't have an eating disorder."

"But you're not eating—"

"That's not why!" There's no way I can tell them. It's just too embarrassing. "I'm . . . there's just some stuff going on. I'll be okay."

They let me leave the table. I hide out in my room for the rest of the night. When I go to bed, I can't fall asleep. I'm all restless and jittery. A warm breeze flows in through my window. Maybe taking a walk will help me get tired enough to sleep.

I put on a T-shirt and shorts and grab my flip-flops. Then I sneak down the stairs, avoiding the creaky one.

When I'm about to open the door, I hear the porch swing's chains clanking. I yank my hand away from the doorknob. Leaning over to the window, I peek out.

Blake's lying on the swing.

I open the door slowly so I don't scare him. He sits up.

"What are you doing here?" I whisper.

"Can I stay here tonight?" Blake asks.

"Why are you—"

"Just can I?"

"Yeah. Of course."

I sit next to him on the swing. We sit like that for a long time before he says anything.

"I can't go home," Blake says. "My dad kicked me out. We had the nastiest fight ever."

"About what?"

"He found out about my locker."

"How?"

"Mr. Bradley called him. Too bad he didn't stop to consider that not every parent is the understanding type."

"I'm so sorry."

"Don't be. Now I don't have to worry about coming out to my dad anymore."

Blake's always been convinced that his dad would kill him if he found out that Blake is gay. I knew his dad would be mad, but I never thought anything like this would happen. What kind of person throws his own kid out of the house?

"I'm never going back there," Blake says. "Do you think I could stay with you for a while? I'll totally pay for food and stuff."

"I'm sure you can. I'll ask my mom in the morning."

Blake stretches out on the swing again, resting his head on a folded blanket he took out of the trunk. "Sorry I was mad at you."

"Seriously? This is all my fault! I can't believe how stupid I was."

"You didn't know Ryan could hear."

"I didn't mean to tell Jason. I am *so* sorry."

"It's like my horoscope said last week. What was it? Something like, 'Information meant to be released can't stay secret forever. Now's the time for change.'"

"See how it always knows?"

"Um, yeah, I think I'm convinced."

I get up and hold my hand out to Blake. "You can't stay out here. Come sleep in my room."

"Won't Jason be jealous?"

"I never knew you could be so funny after midnight."

Inflating the air mattress would be too noisy, so I get my sleeping bag out. I put a fresh pillowcase on one of my pillows for Blake.

"Take the bed," I go.

"No, I'll take the floor."

"*Take* the *bed*."

"You run a tight ship around here."

Blake gets into my bed and falls asleep right away. I'm still strung out on the adrenaline rush from finding him on my porch in the middle of the night. How can he just fall asleep like that?

In the morning, I find Mom washing vegetables in the kitchen.

"Mom?"

"Oh!" She drops a beet in the sink. "You scared me."

"Sorry."

"Do you want a sandwich or leftovers for lunch?" Mom asks. I told her I wanted to start bringing my lunch instead of buying. When she asked why, I said it's because the skanky school lunches are wrecking my health. Which is true.

"Um, a sandwich is okay."

She goes back to washing vegetables.

"Mom?"

"What is it, honey?"

"We need to talk."

We sit at the kitchen table. I tell her there's a rumor about Blake. I tell her about his locker and how his dad threw him out. I leave out the part about my telling Jason that Blake is gay.

"So Blake can stay here, right?" I go.

"That poor boy."

"I told him it would probably be okay."

"I don't think that's such a good idea."

"Why not?"

"Blake's dad can't just force him out of his home. That's illegal. We should probably tell the police. Or child protective services— I'll have to look into it."

"Why can't he just stay here for a while?"

"If his dad refuses to take him back, the authorities might want him to stay with another relative."

Staying with another relative isn't the easiest solution when there's only one possibility. Blake's uncle is the only other family he has. Blake told me about Uncle Rick. He's a construction worker who chops wood for people before the winter and grows Christmas trees to sell in the city.

I go, "But his uncle is the closest relative and he lives, like, an hour away."

"Well, Blake might have to move in with him."

"No way! Then he'd have to transfer to another school."

Mom just shakes her head.

"This sucks," I say.

"Let's see what happens with Blake's dad first. Things like this tend to blow over after a few days."

"It's not fair that he can't stay here."

"We have to do what's best for Blake."

I glare at her. "Really? Because it sounds more like you're doing what's best for you."

Upstairs, I roll up my sleeping bag. When Blake gets out of the shower he comes back to my room, rubbing a towel over his hair.

"How are you feeling?" I ask.

"Good."

"Good?"

"Yeah."

"This might be a stupid question, but why?"

"Don't you get it? I don't have to be afraid anymore. I don't have to dread what's going to happen when my dad finds out. If this is the worst of it, then I got off easy."

"What about everyone at school?"

"They're dumbasses. I don't have time for ignorance."

Blake's handling this way better than I thought he would. Either he's having some sort of mental breakdown or he worked through this super quickly.

He goes, "Did you talk to your mom?"

I get busy tying up the sleeping bag. "Um-hm."

"What'd she say?"

"She said . . ." I stop tying. "She said no."

"What? Why?"

"Because she's being impossible." I'm so mad at Mom for not letting Blake stay. In retaliation, I'm planning to take an extra-long shower and leave the bathroom light on when I'm done.

"Am I at least allowed to stay here tonight?" Blake says.

"I can try to ask for one more night, but . . ."

"Damn," Blake says. "What am I supposed to do now?"

38

The best poster I made for One World was ripped to shreds.

It took me two hours to make. The lettering was pristine. I used eight different colors of glitter. I even made cool graphics and glued them on.

Someone yanked the poster down. They ripped it up. They threw the pieces all over the floor.

I pick up one of the pieces. It has an Earth Jason made on our arts-and-crafts night. I used the Earth for the "*o*" in "*World*." I decorated it with green and blue glitter. Our glitter Earth was perfect.

Too bad the real Earth isn't.

I can't handle the cafeteria. Just because we're not allowed to go off campus for lunch doesn't mean I have to eat in there. I'm planning to avoid lunch entirely by doing club stuff or going to the library instead. Staying busy is key.

Today I'm eating lunch under the stairs. I really needed some alone time. If someone catches me, who cares? It's not like they can humiliate me any more than they already have.

Blake would eat with me, but he's not here today. My mom gave in and let him sleep over one more night. Uncle Rick came to pick him up this morning.

After talking about it with Dad, Mom called child protective services to make an anonymous report. They said that verbal abuse can be as serious as physical abuse. All types of abuse have lasting emotional damage. Blake's dad has been verbally abusing Blake for as long as he can remember. No one should have to live like that.

So Uncle Rick arranged for Blake to stay with him until college. I'm not sure what's going to happen to his dad. I'm just so relieved that Blake doesn't have to live with him anymore. Uncle Rick lives forty-five minutes away and works in the opposite direction, so Blake has to take the train to school and back. They're moving Blake's stuff today while his dad's at work.

While Blake and I were watching a movie last night, Jason kept calling. At first I didn't pick up. I knew that if I talked to him, it would be even harder to keep my promises to Erin. But his messages said that he was going to keep calling until I talked to him. Blake said Jason was already suffering enough and why couldn't I at least hear what he had to say? So the next time Jason called, I picked up, walking to my room.

"You answered," Jason went.

"I promised Erin I wouldn't talk to you."

"I know. I have to talk to you anyway. Can I come over?"

"No! She'll never trust me again—I told her last week that I wouldn't see you or anything."

"She doesn't have to know."

"*I'll* know."

"Is she more important than me?"

"That's not fair."

"What's staying away from me going to prove? She already knows we were together this summer."

"That's no reason to make it worse."

Silence.

"You know I feel horrible about everything," I say. "I hate that things are like this."

"Then why do they have to be?"

"Because she's my best friend! That's how it is!"

"No, that's the way you're making it. It can be any way we want."

"So, what, being with me right now sounds like a good idea to you? Being seen together in school, in front of Erin? Torturing her even more than we already have? We're supposed to walk down the hall holding hands and eat lunch together like last year and then you can drive me home from school?"

"Um. Yeah."

"No way! That would make everything so much worse!"

"You don't want to be with me?"

"Of course I want to be with you! You know I do."

"I used to. But I'm not sure anymore."

All this time, I was so concerned about how I was hurting

Erin that I didn't stop to think about how all of this was affecting Jason. Of course I knew we were both miserable. But when I said I couldn't be with him, he agreed even though he didn't want to. That's how much he cares about me.

"I don't want things to be like this," Jason said. "But more than anything, I want you to be happy. If it's going to make you miserable to be with me, then I'll stay away."

"That's not what I'm saying."

"It kind of is."

That was the worst conversation ever. Not only am I hurting Erin, I'm hurting Jason, too.

I was thinking that it was impossible for things to get any worse until Communications. The good thing about this class is that it's in the computer lab. You can totally get away with doing stuff you're not supposed to be doing. Bonus: We have a sub today who's giving us free online time.

Except free online time is not the break from reality I was hoping for. I want to float away in an online bubble until school's over. Only, that's kind of hard to do when people keep laughing. And looking at me. I mean, whatever, people have been laughing and looking at me forever. But they're obviously laughing and looking for a more specific reason this time.

I glance at one of the computer screens on the table in front of mine. Am I crazy, or am I seeing a picture of myself? Online. A horrible picture I would never post anywhere.

An IM pops up on my screen. It says:

Want to see?

There's a link. I click it. When the website comes up, I'm immediately nauseated. I was assuming they wouldn't be this obscene.

I was wrong.

The website is called Committee Against Sluts. Underneath the horrible picture is the caption, LANI IS A SLUT.

In between more pictures, there are comments about how I'm disgusting and can't get my own boyfriend so I have to steal one from my best friend. One comment is about how I think I'm so righteous for saving the planet, when everyone knows I'm just doing it to get into a good college. This other girl (I'm sure a girl wrote this because only girls could be this catty) ranted about every supposedly conceited thing I ever did, all the way back to middle school. I can tell by some of the things she wrote that it was Danielle.

Danielle actually wrote this.

She was my friend.

So which one did Erin write? Is she the one who started this website? It's impossible to tell who started it. Maybe a bunch of people did. Now that it's out there and everyone's seen it, there's nothing I can do.

My heart hurts. How can someone who means so much to a person mean nothing the next day? I thought that Erin would always be there for me, no matter what. I thought that was the one true thing I could count on.

This just proves how quickly your life can be destroyed. Even when you think things couldn't possibly get any worse.

39

It's been a week since I saw the website. A week of knowing everyone saw it. Another week of Erin and Danielle ignoring me. Another week of avoiding Jason, which is the hardest thing of all.

What if this nightmare never ends? What if this is my life from now on?

My grades suck. I haven't been able to concentrate on any work this year. Mr. Bradley called me into his office so we could talk about how much my grades suck. That was fun. I had to promise to do better before he let me go. Not that it matters. I seem to be an expert on breaking promises these days.

As soon as history is over, Connor sprints to my desk before I can escape.

"I have to show you something," he goes.

"What?"

"Not here. What do you have now?"

"Lunch." I'm back to eating in the cafeteria again. Blake forgave me, so I've been sitting with him and the art crowd. They adopted Blake due to his impressive glassblowing skills. They're actually a really interesting group. I'm glad that I'm getting to know them before we graduate.

"Come on." Connor directs me down the hall toward the science wing.

I'm like, "Where are we going?"

"It's a secret."

"What do you have now?"

"English."

"You're cutting English for this?"

"Some things are more important."

Then something amazing happens. Connor brings me to my secret staircase and pulls me under the stairs.

"Shut up!" I go.

"Sshhh!"

"How do you know about this place?" I whisper.

"Doesn't everybody?"

"No! I thought I was the only one!"

"Well, you're not." Connor takes out a note. "Jason asked me to give you this."

Jason won't let go. He hasn't called me all week. But I know he's determined to get me back. I just knew he wouldn't give up.

I'm afraid of what his note says. I'm afraid it's going to make me want to be with him even more.

"Oh." I take the note. "Thanks. I'll, um . . . read it later." I push the note into my back pocket.

"There's something else I want to show you." Connor rummages in his bag. He takes out a ragged notebook. "This was my journal a few years ago."

"You have a journal?"

"American guys don't really do that, eh?"

"And? They also don't call their sweatpants *jogging pants*. American guys are clearly lacking."

"They could improve. All they need is some sensitivity."

"Like that's going to happen." This is one thing I love about Jason. He's sensitive and not afraid to show it. Most guys would be humiliated to even expose a fraction of a feeling. Jason's not like that.

Hence, the note in my pocket.

Connor flips through his journal. He shows me a page. It's all in French.

"What's it say?" I ask.

"This thing with you and Jason reminded me of something. There was this café across the street from my old place in Montreal. I always liked to sit at the same table in the window, you know? All the tables had these white paper tablecloths that you could draw on. One day I went in and someone had written this on my tablecloth."

Connor translates the message from his journal. It's about a person who doesn't know who his soul mate is, but he's looking for her. He will never give up. When they find each other, they will know. It says how you have to follow your heart to find true love.

"See this line here?" Connor points to a part that says:

Rien ne va arrêter ma quête pour te trouver.

"I was just overwhelmed by the intensity of it," Connor tells me. "It says, 'Nothing will stop my quest to find you.' This person will keep going forever if he has to. But you and Jason have already found each other. You're obviously meant to be together, but you're not together. That's a problem, no?"

Of course he's right. Of course it's a problem. And of course he wrote down that message for a reason. He was obviously meant to tell me what it said. Fate made sure that the message got to me from a whole other country.

It can't be easy for Connor to be telling me all of this. I know how he feels about me. I also know that he's been concerned about how miserable I am. It's like he's pushing aside his own feelings out of respect for mine. That's the kind of person he is.

"Thanks for this," I say. "It's probably not the easiest thing for you."

"No, it's not. I almost didn't show this to you, actually. But I just . . . want you to be happy."

That's exactly what Jason said. He just wants me to be happy.

Of course, the only thing that could make me happy is the one thing I can't have. I want to be with Jason more than anything. But I can't break my promise to Erin.

She has to forgive me. I know it won't be easy and I know I might have to wait a really long time, but Erin has to forgive me. Which is never going to happen if I can't prove to her that our friendship means more than being with Jason.

When I get home, I unfold Jason's note. It's in his secret note code.

Decoded, the note says:

I need you so much closer.

40

When you're a senior, you're supposed to be psyched that everything will finally be over soon. I wish I could be happy like everyone else. It's just not registering with me. Eight months from now does not equal "soon." June is a lifetime away.

I thought senior year would be a lot different. All of us together, having a blast. Not caring about homework or grades after college apps are in. Focusing on the things that really matter.

This is nothing like that.

Connor gave me that note from Jason two weeks ago. I've been crying every night, aching for him.

As if I don't have enough problems, I can't find my English paper that's due today. It's supposed to be right here in my binder. I even finished it a day early since I had nothing better to do.

I rip my binder apart looking for it. Still nothing.

After I've dumped about half the contents of my locker on the floor, I find a random note behind some books. It's one of Jason's secret-code notes from last year. I have no idea how it got in my locker, since I thought I had all of his notes in a special box at home.

The Energy is *so* giving me a sign right now.

But maybe not. So I put the note in a folder. I go back to searching for my missing English paper. I crouch down and sift through everything on the floor.

Someone walks up to me. And just stands there.

I totally recognize those sneakers.

"Hey," Jason says.

It feels so good to hear him talking to me.

I'm too scared to look at him.

Jason helps me pick everything up. "What happened here? One of those weird earthquakes that only affects half the hall?"

"Something like that."

"How are you?"

"Sad." I stuff things back into my locker. I can't even remember what I was looking for.

"Me, too," Jason says.

I finally look at him. He looks like he hasn't slept in days.

"I can't do this anymore," Jason says. "I can't be away from you."

Some kids have been watching us ever since Jason came over. I'm sure they're discussing how scandalous this is. *Oh look, not only did Lani steal Jason away from Erin, but now she's flirting with him in front of the whole school. What a monster.*

"People are looking," I whisper.

"I don't care," he says. "We have to be together."

My throat's all tight. It's not letting me say what I really want to say.

Jason moves closer. "Erin already knows. She already got hurt. Do you really think she wants you to be this miserable?"

"She's not going to be this mad forever. We just need to give her time."

"This isn't about her anymore. It's about us." Jason pulls me closer to him. "And I don't care who knows."

Then he kisses me.

Right here, in the middle of the hall, with everyone looking.

He kisses me.

I thought I remembered what it felt like to kiss him. But this is unreal.

Jason says, "I love you."

Everyone watching us stopped talking when he kissed me. Which means a whole bunch of people just heard Jason say that he loves me.

"Stop being like this," Jason goes. "What are you so afraid of?"

I'm totally shocked. Way too shocked to say anything.

Everyone's staring. Some of my stuff is still on the floor. I'm late for class.

"Um . . ." I quickly scoop up the rest of my stuff, throw it in my locker, and slam the door. My hand shakes as I click my lock shut. "I'm late for class."

I know Jason wants me to say that I love him, too. And that

we should be together and I don't care what Erin thinks anymore. But this is just too much.

Jason watches me, waiting to hear the things I can't say. Walking away from him is the last thing I want to do, but I don't see any other way.

Being late for English is not fun. Ms. Bigelow makes this whole production of taking off points if you're late. Not that it matters. My English grade is so bad that a few more points off will hardly make a dent.

Ms. Bigelow is like, "I've already collected the papers." She waits for me to pass mine up. So now I have to admit that I can't find mine. There's no way she's going to believe me.

"I can't find mine," I say.

"I'm sorry?" Ms. Bigelow goes, even though she totally heard me.

"It was in my binder, but now I can't find it. That's why I was late."

"That's too bad."

She doesn't believe me. She starts the lesson anyway.

I don't know exactly what makes me start crying. Maybe it's the frustration of knowing that I really did my paper, but now I look like a liar all over again. Maybe it's how Jason kissed me and told me he loves me in front of everyone and I just walked away. Or maybe it's coming to school every single day with so many people still hating me. That can wear a person down.

Of course I always have a pack of Sniff tissues in my bag except for today. I can't stop crying, even though I'm telling myself to quit it.

Ms. Bigelow stops teaching. She says, "Lani? Are you all right?"

I nod. I try to look like I'm calming down. But her asking me just makes it worse.

Someone in the back does this snorting-laugh thing.

Ms. Bigelow picks up the bathroom pass and gives it to the person sitting in the front of my row. "Pass this back, please." When Marnie turns to give me the pass, she's totally smirking. No one feels bad for me. They're probably all thinking, *This is what you get for being such a slut. Oh, and we don't believe you about your paper.*

What if Erin never forgives me? What if I stay away from Jason and it's all for nothing?

Maybe everything that happens in our lives isn't already decided by fate. Maybe we have some influence over the outcome. If you want something badly enough, can you change your fate? Or will the thing you want the most come true anyway, no matter what you do?

41

Blake finally had a decent day at school.

Ryan Campanelli got in trouble for spray-painting his locker.

I was worried that whoever did it would get away with it because nothing was ever proven. But Sophie totally turned Ryan in. Ryan was suspended for a week. He should have been expelled, but his mother's on the school board.

Sophie suspected that Ryan was the one who did it, but she didn't have any proof. So she kept watching Ryan to see if he'd screw up. When a pile of books slid out of Ryan's locker in between classes, Sophie looked in and saw a spray-paint can wedged in the back. She went over and yanked the can out of Ryan's locker. Of course it was the same shade of yellow used on Blake's locker.

"You're the one who spray-painted Blake's locker!" Sophie yelled. She held the can up so everyone could see.

The hall got quiet. Everyone stared at them.

Ryan looked around at everyone staring. He knew it would be pointless to deny it.

"So?" Ryan went.

"How could you do something like that? It's disgusting, even for you."

Some of the kids who were watching snickered.

Ryan was all, "Who cares? People were talking about him last year. It's not like I outed him or anything."

Sophie got right in his face. "Um, actually? You did."

Then Sophie asked why Ryan waited so long to do anything if he knew about Blake since last year. Ryan didn't have to explain anything to her. He could have just walked away. But in some warped way, I think he's proud of what he did. So Ryan said that if he told people last year before school ended or during the summer, it wouldn't have had the same impact. He wanted to wait until the first day of school and slam Blake with the full force of everyone talking about it at once. That way, Blake would be burned way harsher than if the rumor trickled out over the summer. Sophie told me Ryan was practically bragging about the whole thing.

It's scary how powerful hate can be.

Taking the train to Uncle Rick's house after school is more fun than I thought it would be. I hate that Blake has to spend so much time alone on the train every day, so I promised I'd go home with him sometimes.

The train rattles. I watch the landscape zipping by. I'm thinking about all of the history here, all of the hidden treasures that might never be discovered. And about how much Jason loves the train tracks. I totally get what he sees in them. It feels like I'm on my way to a new destination. A place I don't really know yet, one I can't see from here. A place I'll recognize from somewhere deep within my soul when I get there.

"So I heard some action went down in the hall today," Blake says.

I groan. "Don't remind me."

"What, you didn't want to be kissed?"

The truth is that Jason's kiss rocked me so hard I'm still shaking. I just can't get into it yet, so I say, "Not in front of everyone, no."

"I talked to Erin."

"You *told* her?!"

"Like I would do that. She'd already heard about it, along with the rest of the world."

I groan some more.

Blake goes, "I talked to her about you and Jason."

"There *is* no me and Jason."

"Exactly. That's the problem."

"You're so annoying."

"Am I? Or are you a little bit crazy?"

"I can't be with Jason when—"

"Yeah, yeah." Blake flutters his hand in my face. "Erin saved your life and now you owe her. But can I just ask—how is staying away from Jason paying her back?"

"I don't want to hurt her any more than I already have."

"Um, it's called life. Erin's a big girl. She can handle it."

"What did you say to her?"

"Just that you can't keep soul mates apart forever."

"You *said* that?!"

"Like it's a lie? Anyway, she has to know by now, she's just not admitting it to herself. It's not like she hasn't seen you guys together."

"What did she say?"

"Nothing. She was leaving and I had to catch the train with you."

This is bad. Really bad. Now Erin probably thinks that I made Blake talk to her. Like I was too afraid to talk to her myself or something.

"No worries," Blake says. "It will all work out the way it's supposed to. If you and Jason are meant to be together, which you obviously are, then it'll happen."

I wish it was that easy.

The good news is that Uncle Rick has an extensive movie collection. Blake and I argue about which one to watch.

"Why can't we watch *The Puffy Chair*?" I say.

"Because it's boring."

"It is not! How can you not think it's so good?"

"Um . . . maybe because it's boring?"

"Do you have a better suggestion?"

"What about *Juno*?"

"I just saw that again, remember?"

"Oh, yeah. Well, how about *The Safety of Objects*?"

"I've seen that, like, five times."

"So? It's still awesome, right?"

"Agreed."

I pop some popcorn while Blake starts the movie. We set up on the couch.

"That's cool." I point to a delicate glass vase on the coffee table.

"Thanks," Blake says. "I made it."

"Dude, you have immense talent."

"Not really. It took me forever."

We watch *The Safety of Objects*. We're blasting the TV since there's no one home to tell us to turn it down. Uncle Rick won't be home from work for at least another hour.

When the door opens, we don't even hear it.

Something moves in my peripheral vision. I grab Blake's arm.

Blake's dad is just standing there.

Watching us.

No one ever locks their doors around here during the day. Especially in an area like this, which is even more remote than ours.

"What are you doing here?" Blake goes.

"I wanted to see you."

"Why? So you can yell at me some more? So you can rant about how worthless I am?"

His dad glances at me. I'm not going anywhere.

Blake goes over to his dad. I'm not sure when it happened, but Blake is taller than him now.

"You," Blake says, "will never hurt me again."

"You lied to me," his dad says.

"When?"

"For years. You said . . . You lied all that time."

"About what?"

His dad doesn't say anything.

"About *what*, Dad?"

"You know what."

"You can't even say it, can you? About me being gay?"

No response.

"Because I'm gay, Dad? Is that your problem? That I didn't tell you? Why do you think I hid it?"

"Hey—" Blake's dad grabs his arm.

Blake shoves his dad back, hard.

"Why do you think?" Blake yells. "Because you'd hate me if you knew! Because you'd say disgusting things to me until I'd wish I were dead!"

His dad stays quiet.

"Do you have any idea what it's like to know your own father hates you?" Blake yells even louder. "You're supposed to love me! That's your job! I'm gay and you can't even say it. You can't admit who I really am."

I want to run over and hug Blake and never let him go. I could not be more impressed with him. He's finally saying all the things he's wanted to say for so long. He's overcome his fear.

Now would be a good time for Blake's dad to tell Blake that he loves him and he's here for him, no matter what. That he accepts Blake for who he is because Blake is his son. That Blake should come home.

Blake's dad doesn't say any of those things.

He just leaves. Just walks right out the door.

"Good thing I have Uncle Rick," Blake says. Then he sits down on the floor and cries.

I go over to Blake and hug him. He's shaking.

"I'm here for you," I say. "Whatever you need."

It's such a relief that Uncle Rick is taking care of Blake. He accepts Blake for who he is unconditionally, the way you're supposed to with family. Uncle Rick respects that Blake's dad is his brother, but he hates the way Blake has been mistreated.

That's the tricky thing about being bonded to someone for life. Blake and his dad are bonded like I'm bonded with Erin. We're irrevocably tied together by history, a history that can never be erased. Even if you want to deny it, even if you want to pretend it never existed, it will always be a part of you. It will always, in some way, define who you are.

42

According to most people, fall starts on the first day of school. I disagree. I think that fall starts when you feel it in the air. Like today, how it's all crisp and cool outside.

It's official. Every last part of summer is over.

It's been hard to stay in my room for more than a few minutes. It's like I can't deal with confined spaces anymore. I need wide open areas, where I can run far away if I have to. That's why I'm doing my homework on the front porch, spread out on the wicker couch with a blanket over my lap.

I think about how Blake stood up to his dad. He was so afraid of his dad for all those years. Then yesterday, everything changed. Blake faced his worst fear. If he hadn't finally confronted his dad, Blake's future would probably be a lot different.

Which means that we do have at least *some* control over our fate. If Blake can finally say all the things he's been keeping in for so long, after so many years of heartache and pain, then I can definitely deal with this. My fear of facing Erin is nothing compared to what Blake went through. I can change my fate just like Blake did.

If I want things to change, I can't just sit around wishing they would change. I have to *make* them change.

I jump up and run inside. When I call Erin, I'm surprised that she actually answers.

"Where are you?" I say.

"Why?"

"Just where are you?"

"The Fountain."

"Meet me at Green Pond in fifteen minutes."

"What do—"

I hang up. This can only be done in person.

Green Pond is too far away for me to get there in time on my bike. Of course Dad's car isn't here, so I have to take the stick.

Driving over to meet Erin, I get angrier by the minute. I'm so angry I stall like seven times. The last time I restart the car, I practically rip the stick shift out and smash it against the windshield.

When I get there, she's already waiting for me. I can't tell anything from her expression.

I slam my door. Hard.

Erin's by the edge of the pond, holding some pebbles. I saw her trying to skim some on the water when I pulled up. Neither one of us has ever been able to master skimming stones. We keep trying anyway.

"Why are you still being like this?" I go.

"Like what?"

"Like someone I don't even know anymore."

Erin drops the pebbles. She brushes her hand on her jeans. "Aren't you the one who stole my boyfriend?"

"No. I started going out with your *ex*-boyfriend *after* he broke up with you. You should really get your facts straight."

"You shouldn't have hooked up with Jason at all. What kind of friend are you?"

"You're so self-centered! The world doesn't revolve around you! *God.* You just . . . you don't realize how you affect people. You never take responsibility for what you do. It's always about what *you* want. Well, guess what? The rest of us want things, too. Not everything is about you!"

I can't believe I just said all that. I wanted to come over here to make up with Erin, not make her even angrier at me.

"I don't have to listen to this," Erin goes. "I'm leaving."

"No!" I grab her arm.

"Ow!"

"Listen!" I say. "I can't apologize anymore! I've already said I'm sorry. There's nothing else I can do. I can't change the way things are. And you know what? Even if I could, I wouldn't want to. I'm sorry that Jason broke up with you. But staying away from him hasn't solved anything."

Erin pulls her arm away.

But she doesn't leave.

She stays.

Erin's been acting like I'm the only one who did something wrong. How about what she did with Jason's email? It's one thing to be mad at your friend. It's a whole other thing to get the rest of the world hating her, too.

"How could you forward Jason's email like that?" I ask.

"I know it was bad. I was just . . . beyond angry."

"It's not fair how everyone hates me."

"I took it to the extreme," Erin says. "I'm sorry."

I watch her turn one of her rings. She's nervous, but trying to hide it. Maybe Erin's not as fearless as I always thought she was.

And that's when I realize how much I miss her. I just miss her so much.

My throat gets all tight. My eyes fill with tears.

"How much longer are you going to let this come between us?" I say. "We were already growing apart way before this. I know you felt it, too."

All of a sudden, Erin starts crying.

"That website thing was wrong," she says. "It shouldn't have happened."

"Did you start it?"

"No. But I know who did. I got her to take it down."

"Who was it?"

"It doesn't matter."

A wave of exhaustion hits me. All of my anger has evaporated, leaving me feeling like a wilted flower.

Erin goes, "I don't like being mad at you."

"I didn't mean to hurt you."

"I know."

"Do you?"

"Yeah. I mean, I get it, but that doesn't make it hurt any less."

"I'm really, really sorry about everything."

"I heard about what happened yesterday."

"That was totally Jason's fault! I told him I didn't want to talk to him or—"

"I know," Erin interrupts. "Here's the thing, though. I don't know how fair that is."

"What do you mean?"

"You want to be with him. And he obviously wants to be with you. So it's not right for me to keep you apart."

"It's—"

"Things with you guys might not work out or whatever, but I don't want you to blame me for not being together."

"You don't hate me anymore?"

Erin smiles a little. It's the first time I've seen her smile since this whole disaster started. "I can't hate you, Lani. There's too much history between us."

This bond that Erin and I have was supposed to mean that we'd always be friends forever. That nothing could ever come between us. Now I'm wondering if our bond is strong enough. Maybe we've grown apart so much that the accident doesn't matter anymore. Maybe the rest of what we have together isn't enough.

I'm not sure if our friendship is strong enough to survive into next year when we're away at college.

But.

We know each other in a way that no one else can. We share a history that makes us permanently connected. So I have hope for us.

All I can do is hope.

43

Erin and I talked for a long time yesterday. We stayed at the pond until it got dark. Even though it was hard for her, she really made an effort to be friends again.

Yesterday I stopped hiding the way I feel. So today, I am free.

I get on my bike and ride to Jason's house. I don't even know if he's home. I just know that I have to be with him.

The plastic flowers on my bike basket flap in the breeze. I zoom down a hill. The flowers flap harder.

When I knock on Jason's door, no one answers. Phil barks from inside. I hear him scratching on the door.

"Don't worry, Phil," I tell him through the door. "It's just me."

Phil stops scratching.

I sit on the front steps, waiting for Jason to come home. A mourning dove hoos. I try to find which tree he's in.

The sun gets lower. Jason's still not home.

Then it hits me. I might know where he is.

I ride to the place he took me right before school started. Jason said it's the best place for walking the train tracks, where he can completely leave the world behind.

I leave my bike next to his Jeep. Then I search the tracks up through the trees. There's a flash of red shirt. I follow the red shirt. I trip on a branch and come crashing through the tall grass.

"Nice entrance," Jason says.

"Really? Because I practiced it *so* many times."

Jason watches me climb up onto the train tracks.

I don't know what I was expecting. I guess I wasn't assuming that everything would be okay. A lot of heavy stuff is still out there. That kiss in the hall. Jason telling me he loves me. Walking away from him. Somehow, despite these things, I was hoping Jason would be relieved that I found my way back to him.

Except he doesn't look relieved. It's more like he's annoyed.

"I'm sorry about what happened," I say. "I shouldn't have walked away like that."

"Then why did you?"

"I was scared. I didn't want to break my promise to Erin. I talked to her yesterday and . . . we haven't exactly worked everything out, but at least she realizes that we should be together."

"She said that?"

"Pretty much, yeah."

"So . . . what now?"

"Now we can be together."

Jason looks into the distance where the train tracks disappear among the trees. "Did you ever consider how I felt when you decided we couldn't see each other anymore?" he said. "Do you have any idea how hard that was for me? Because it really hurt, Lani. I agreed to it because I hated to see you so sad. But you never asked me what I wanted."

"I know. I'm sorry about that, but I couldn't see any other way for us to be together."

"We should have figured it out, both of us. You shut me out. It's like nothing is ever enough for you. I tell you I love you and you just walk away. How could you do that?"

There's this panicked feeling in my stomach. Jason was trying to convince me that we should be together despite Erin. Now I have to convince him that I can be in a real relationship.

"I've never had a boyfriend before," I say. "I don't really know how to handle some things yet. Trust me, I didn't mean for it to be so one-way between us. I shouldn't have decided everything by myself. Being with you is all that matters. You have to know that."

Jason reaches his hand out to me. "Come on," he says.

We walk down the train tracks, into the distance where they disappear into the trees. Our destination isn't clear. All I know is that I want to get there together.

The Unknown is scary. I'll always have some fear about what's going to happen next. The thing is, the Unknown can also be exciting. Your life could change in an instant anytime. But sometimes, that change is the best thing that will ever happen to you.

Maybe I don't have to know what my fate is to know that everything will be okay. Maybe the not knowing is how we move forward. Wherever I'm headed, I know it's exactly where I'm supposed to be.

Jason ♡

1423 Green Pond Road

Newfoundland, NJ 07438

Dear Jason,

Words aren't enough to make you understand how much I miss you. So I'll have to wait and show you when I get home.

In the ocean today, I saw a million tropical fish. The water is so clear! Thanks for never giving up on me. You always said you could teach me how to swim. You have magical powers.

See you really soon.
Love from Hawaii,
Lani

Acknowledgments

From the instant Lani began telling me her story, I've had a very good feeling about this book. Creating a book is always a team effort, so I want to thank the members of my team.

The Sun

None of this would have been possible without my Penguin family. I would like to especially thank Kendra Levin and Regina Hayes, my magnificent editors. Their talent, sensitivity, and insight ensured that this book was shaped into the best version of itself. Warm fuzzies also go out to Jillian Laks, Karen Chaplin, Eileen Kreit, Janet Pascal, Abigail Powers, Susan Casel, Jim Hoover, Jana Singer, Samantha Dell'Olio, Courtney Wood, Kim Pranschke, and Emily Romero.

The World

Books that can help readers improve their lives in both big and small ways make this world a better place. These are the kinds of books I hope to write. My motivation to write for teens was sparked by books that spoke to me in amazing ways. I want to thank the authors who first inspired me to consider helping readers the way they helped me. Eternal thanks to Louise Fitzhugh, Sandra Scoppettone, Judy Blume, Shel Silverstein, and S.E. Hinton. When I felt like I was completely alone, their books were true friends.

The Star

Thanks to my agents, Gillian MacKenzie and Kirsten Wolf, who make magic happen. And ultimate thanks to Pierre, who always believes in me, even when I don't.